To:

you for your support!

Tiu-Loo:

No Bad Deed Goes Unpunished

Tiu-Loo:

No Bad Deed Goes Unpunished

By

Antonio "T'No" Johnson

Copyright © 2021 Antonio Johnson

All In All Publishing
1893 Hidden Water Drive
Memphis, TN 38134
www.allinallpublishing.com

ISBN # 978-1-953090-16-4

Printed in the United States of America

First Printing, 2021

Front cover image by TB Oatis.
Book design by All In All Publishing.

All rights reserved. No part of this publication may be reproduced, distributed, or transmitted in any form or by any means, including photocopying, recording, or other electronic or mechanical methods, without the prior written permission of the publisher, except in the case of brief quotations embodied in critical reviews and certain other noncommercial uses permitted by copyright law. For permission requests, write to the publisher, addressed "Attention: Permissions Coordinator," at the address above.

"It's a lot of real G's doin' time. Cause a groupie bent the TRUTH and told a LIE!"

-Tupac Amaru Shakur

Acknowledgements

To the millions of men around the world who are and have been falsely imprisoned: remember to keep the faith and your head held high. Tough times never last but tough people do. Also remember this, telling or saying the same LIE over and over still doesn't make it true.

-Jah Bless!

Table of Contents

Prologue

"Like seriously, what are you up to?" asked Tiu-Loo. He had been picked up by his friend, Gator, about an hour ago. It was a slightly warm and breezy day in Havana, Cuba. The air was fresh, and Tiu-Loo was a bit relieved to have been rescued by his good friend. Although he had shown up unannounced, Tiu-Loo was always happy to see Gator. "Oh relax, asere. It's a surprise!" said Gator with a smile on his face. Tiu-Loo had been doing an estimate with a client who had been unsure for several weeks of whether he wanted to purchase the property or not. It was a potential close every time they met, but Tiu-Loo felt like the man was wasting his time. On the brink of frustration, Gator pulled up in his Ford F-150, and told Tiu-Loo to get in with him.

Tiu-Loo stared out of the window. His long, flowing dreadlocks swung back and forth, as they continued to drive to their destination. "Hey, before we get there, I'm gonna need you to put this blind fold on," said Gator. As he processed what was being requested of him, Tiu-Loo promptly replied, "Oh, hell no! For what reason!?" Gator burst into laughter as he couldn't take Tiu-Loo seriously. The look on his face made the situation even more comical. He wouldn't blink or crack a smile until Gator gave him a valid reason to do what he had asked of him. Gator explained to him that he would just have to trust him, and to follow instructions. Reluctant at first, Tiu-Loo rubbed his bracelet that was on his wrist and carefully put the blind fold on.

They drove for what seemed like forever, but only 27 minutes had passed. When they arrived, Gator walked to the passenger side of the truck. "Alright, step out and put your hands on my shoulders." Gator instructed. Tiu-Loo carefully stepped out one foot at a time and stood up. As they walked, there were a set of steps that they had to clear before they could make it to the door. The path seemed awfully familiar to Tiu-Loo, but he continued to follow Gator. Once they made it to the front door, Gator knocked three times and then shouted, "Hey yo, let me in!" As the door opened, the aroma from an obvious preparation of food had filled Tiu-Loo's nostrils.

"SURPRISE!" everyone shouted, as Tiu-Loo jumped in utter shock from the unexpected noise. He took off the blind fold and stood in amazement and disbelief. It was a room full of employees and a few new, close friends. He still couldn't process what the fuss was all about. He was excited, but nervous at the same time. As he began to wrap his head around what was taking place, a beautiful, and very pregnant woman waddled over to him, giving him a huge hug and big kiss. "Congratulations, Papi. I'm so proud of you!" she said as she looked into his eyes and smiled at him. Esmerelda was his wife of four years and was due to have their new baby within the next few weeks. When Tiu-Loo had arrived in Cuba, Gator kept telling him about his eye-dropping little sister, and how he wanted to introduce him to her. They met, and the rest was history.

"What's all of this for, my love?" Tiu-Loo asked as he grabbed a chair to help his wife take a seat. "It's a celebration. You've been working so hard, and you've finally expanded your construction company." Esmerelda explained. Tiu-Loo embraced his wife, and then rubbed and kissed her belly. "You just hold tight in there, little man. Tell mommy to stay off her feet." He didn't want his wife moving around much while she was pregnant, because he felt that it would cause unnecessary strain and stress. Esmerelda rubbed her hands through Tui-Loo's hair and whispered in his ear, "You've got another surprise waiting on you tonight, so be ready." But they both knew exactly what she meant.

"Now, let's drink and party, shall we!?" Gator shouted as he put one arm around Tiu-Loo. He had explained to Tiu-Loo that they had been planning a surprise party to celebrate his many accomplishments. The most recent being the expansion of his new construction company. He had started a year prior with about ten employees. Before the end of the year, he had reached a total of fifteen new contracts and over 150 employees, staff, and workers. Gator got with his little sister, and devised a plan to surprise his good friend, and it worked.

Tiu-Loo grabbed a beer and asked Gator to help his wife into the bedroom. A few of his close business partners and clients greeted him with gifts and praises. He had been working so hard and was so determined, that he hadn't had time to sit back and look at how much he had achieved since being in Cuba. He just knew that he didn't want to fail, and most importantly, he didn't want to get caught. He took a few sips of his beer, grabbed a rubber band from his pocket to pin his hair, and began to dance to the bachata music that was playing on the speaker. There was nothing but pure joy and great energy occurring at that moment.

The guests began to leave, and Tiu-Loo thanked everyone for a wonderful time. It had been many years since he'd had a good time and could truly relax and enjoy himself. As the final guest exited the home, Gator made his way to the kitchen. Tiu-Loo had finally finished the bottle of beer that he had started on when the party had begun earlier. He was a bit emotional, as he tried to take everything in all at once. "Hey, you deserve everything. Don't even think about the past. This is your new life now, and you're blessed beyond words, compadre," said Gator as he embraced Tiu-Loo. Tiu-Loo didn't say a word. He just let tears flow down his face. His feelings and emotions had overcome him. They knew why the night was so important, and there was no need to elaborate on what they were feeling. It was already understood.

"Now, go get some rest. I'll see you tomorrow. Chao pescao!" Gator said, as he prepared to head home. Tiu-Loo straightened his face and headed upstairs to his bedroom. His house and bedroom were enormous. He had a beautiful Basquiat painting in his living room, a swimming pool, gym, three bathrooms, and six bedrooms. The marble countertops had an earth-tone look, and the winding staircase was Esmerelda's idea.

As he made it upstairs, he sat his phone on the dresser and stepped out onto the balcony of his master bedroom. He closed his eyes as he let the breeze flow through his body. As he began to relax, his phone started ringing. Esmerelda grabbed the phone and answered. "Hello, who is this?" There was a brief hesitation, then the person replied, "Yes, is Chase, I mean Tiu-Loo around?" Esmerelda was taken aback. Absolutely no one called Tiu-Loo by his first name unless they knew him personally. "Yes, hold for one second, please." She walked to the balcony and handed Tiu-Loo the phone. "It's for you, Papi," she said.

As she walked out, Tiu-Loo slowly raised the phone to his ear. "Asere que bola?" he asked as he answered the phone. "What up boy-boy!?" the person asked. Tiu-Loo's eyes widened, and his heart began to beat rapidly. He hadn't heard those words in over five years. It was his best friend Kato. "Hey, how the hell did you find me?" Tiu-Loo asked looking concerned. It wasn't that he didn't want to hear from his old friend, but no one knew of his whereabouts since he had left his hometown; not even Kato.

"Hey, I'm not calling with any drama. I just want you to know that I'm glad you're okay, and I'm glad that you're alive. I wish you nothing but greatness, King. I love you." "I love you, too, boy-boy." Tiu-Loo replied. With that brief transaction of words, the conversation ended. They both hung up and Tiu-Loo stared at the phone for a few seconds. Although the conversation was brief. He was both relieved and in good spirits knowing that his childhood friend was doing fine. "Who was that Papi?" Esmeralda asked as she stood in the doorway of their bedroom. "It was just my cousin Travis, my Uncle Kobe's son," he replied. She scratched her head and was bewildered. From her understanding, his Uncle Kobe didn't have any children. She refrained from asking a follow up question and just nodded. "Now let's get you in the bed. You know I don't want you up on your feet too long," Tiu-Loo said. They made their way inside and fell asleep as the wind blew gently across their bodies.

Chapter 1: Cooties

"Now make sure you tie those shoes correctly." That was Uncle Kobe's final words to little Chase before walking out of Chase's bedroom and heading to his own to prepare for work. It was an early morning and the new school year had already started. It would be Chase's first day of kindergarten, and he was not a happy camper at all. "Uncle Kobe, I don't wanna go," he said, as he kicked his shoes off and sat on the floor. He had been used to doing home activities and learning his numbers and letters with his uncle. The last thing he wanted to do was enter a world where he wouldn't see any familiar faces.

He folded his arms and began to pout. School was the was the furthest thing on his mind. Seeing the distress on Chase's face, Uncle Kobe went over to him and asked him a series of questions. "Now, how old are you? He asked. "I'm five years old." Chase replied in a bit of a mumble. Uncle Kobe instructed him to stand up as he continued to question him. "Tell me, what is your name?" "My name is Chase Marley Carter!" he said with a boast of confidence. Uncle Kobe reminded him of the promise that he had made. He promised Chase that if he were to go to school, and follow the instructions, he would take him to the zoo that following weekend. Chase loved lions and tigers, so he didn't want to miss out on that opportunity.

"I'm scared, Uncle Kobe," he said as he looked him square in the eyes. Uncle Kobe grabbed him and told him that there was nothing to be afraid of. He helped him button up his white shirt, and helped him tuck it into his brown, khaki pants. Chase had a nice amount of hair on his head. They were dreadlocks that stopped right above the middle of his neck. His mother, Lameenah, made his uncle promise to never cut Chase's hair until he was old enough to make that decision for himself.

She was a natural herbalist who would make candles, oils, and skin creams for people in the neighborhood. She would even sell her goods at local and other markets out of town when she could. Her long, flowing locs extended far beyond her hips, and she would wear her hair in a headwrap to prevent them from blinding her as they would fall in front of her face at times. One day, on a trip to New York, she met and briefly fell in love with an African merchant. They would spend many nights together and even made plans to move back to Africa to start a family. The romance would be short lived however, when it was determined that the man, Deyamo, was in America illegally and was eventually deported.

Lameenah was extremely heart broken. Not only was the love of her life taken away, but she was also three months pregnant and about to be a single mother. Luckily, she had a pretty good support system. A tomboy at heart, she had the help of her three brothers. Uncle Kobe was the oldest and the one she was closest to. After finding out that she was having a son, she immediately began to make things for him. Before the end of her second trimester, she had hand crafted shoes, necklaces, and bracelets for her unborn son. She was extremely excited to welcome her bundle of joy into the world.

"Do you want to tie your hair up?" Uncle Kobe asked, as he had Chase follow him into the kitchen for breakfast. "No, I'm fine," Chase replied. The pep talk seemed to work. His frown changed and he moved in more of an upbeat rhythm than he did earlier. With all the persuading and convincing that Uncle Kobe was trying to do, he had forgotten that Chase had kicked his shoes off and had yet to put them back on. "You stay here, I'll be right back," he said, as he went into the bedroom to retrieve the shoes.

Chase opened the pantry door and grabbed a stool. Nothing was going to keep him from getting his early dose of his favorite cereal, Honey Grahams. He pulled the stool close to the pantry door and proceeded to go after the box of cereal. As soon as he was about to reach glory, a voice that he was all too familiar with spoke to him. "Get your black ass down from there, right now!" It was his Uncle Kobe's girlfriend, Dory.

She had been an exotic dancer for many years. She tried a career in video modeling, but her attitude made artists refuse to work with her. She was a light-skinned woman with hazel eyes and freckles. She had a very snappy mouth and voiced her opinion many times, even when no one would ask for it. Uncle Kobe was almost 40 years old, while she was a mere 25. Not long after a few nights spent, Uncle Kobe decided to let her move in with him and Chase.

Things were smooth for a few weeks, but ultimately, she began to show her true colors. Each day, Dory would remind Chase of how dark he was. There would always be a barrage of insults ranging from his dark skin tone to his dark hair. After antagonizing him, she would make him promise not to tell his uncle. A piece of candy or a new video game would be her way of keeping him quiet, but it would always hurt his feelings. It was a rather interesting process, because she would only mistreat him whenever his uncle wasn't around.

Startled, Chase looked back to ask her why he had to get down from the stool. Dory snarled and replied, "Because I said so, that's why. Now get down! Where are your shoes? Aren't you supposed to be going to school today?" Chase ignored her questions while walking over to the kitchen table. "Alright, here we go little man. Let's get your shoes on," Uncle Kobe said, as he walked into the kitchen. Chase sat down in one of the chairs as Uncle Kobe helped him put his shoes on. "Do you remember how we practiced tying your shoes?" Uncle Kobe asked. "Yes sir. Loop, swoop, and pull, right?" Chase asked.

Uncle Kobe nodded his head and gave Chase a high five

for knowing the correct answer. "Uncle Kobe, I want some cereal," Chase said while looking over at the pantry. Before Uncle Kobe could reply, Dory had already stepped in. "I was just about to ask you if you were hungry. Why didn't you say anything?" she asked. Chase gave her a blank stare and looked puzzled. Uncle Kobe even scratched his head for a second, because he was aware that Chase knew how to grab the stool and make a bowl of cereal for himself.

As she poured the cereal, Uncle Kobe went over and hugged Dory from behind. She whispered something into his ear and they both began to laugh. He handed Chase the bowl of cereal and started his timer. "I'm about to go warm the car up, and then it's off to school," Uncle Kobe said. Chase dove into his breakfast with no hesitation. Only five minutes had passed, and he was sipping the last of the milk from the bowl. "Damn, you eat like a dog," Dory uttered as she sparked a cigarette and walked out of the kitchen. It didn't matter what she had said, because for those few minutes, Chase had been in cereal heaven.

He put his bowl in the sink and darted into the living room to get his backpack. He had his school supplies but wanted to take a few of his action figure toys with him. Uncle Kobe came back inside to make sure Chase was ready for the big day. "Your new day is about to begin man! Are you ready?" he asked. Chase held up one of his action figures and looked at Uncle Kobe. "Okay, but you can only take one," he said, as he smiled down at Chase. Excited to be obliged by his uncle, Chase rushed to put the toy into his backpack before Uncle Kobe could change his mind.

They walked outside and got into the car. Chase was a little short for his five-year old frame, so Uncle Kobe always made him sit in the back seat. It didn't bother him much, because he loved having the window down and staring at the trees as they drove by. Besides, the Alabama mornings were rather warm around spring and summer time. As they headed to Chase's school, Uncle Kobe asked him to choose a nursery rhyme to sing. It was something they had done each morning since Chase's second birthday.

Chase instantly started singing "Three Blind Mice." Uncle Kobe chimed in and began to sing along with him. Chase sang on and off beat as his uncle laughed at his attempts to out sing him. Before the fourth attempt of the song, they had already arrived at the school. Chase wasn't ready to go in just yet. He peeped above the car window, just enough to see what was going on. He couldn't believe his eyes. Children were swarming in large numbers as they entered the school building. Of course, he had been around a few children in his neighborhood, but it was nothing compared to what he was seeing at that very moment.

He realized that the other boys were wearing the same white top and khaki pants as he was. The little girls had on red or blue checkered skirts, with white tops to match as well. When one of the students stopped by the car to wave at Chase, he quickly ducked his head down and hoped that he would become invisible. "Now there, you have nothing to be afraid of. I'm sure you'll make a lot of friends today," said Uncle Kobe. He assured Chase that once he relaxed, the day would be as easy as pie for him. Chase smiled and got his backpack ready. It was time to meet his new teacher.

As they entered the school building, Uncle Kobe held Chase's hand as he greeted the new teachers and school principal. It was a yearly tradition for the staff and faculty to greet the new students. It would help build confidence and a strong foundation for the newcomers. Chase was in awe of what he was seeing. The teachers all seemed to be very polite and had big smiles on their faces. He continued to hold on to his uncle as they made their way towards the end of the hallway.

Outside of each teacher's class was a list of students' names on the wall. "Let's see who your teacher is," said Uncle Kobe, as he guided Chase next to him. He put his finger on the paper and scrolled down. Chase was the ninth student listed out of a group of 26. "Looks like you're in Mrs. Sandel's class, little man," Uncle Kobe explained. He gave a light knock on the classroom door and waited for Chase's teacher to let him in. She opened the door and had the biggest smile on her face.

"How are you? I'm Mrs. Sandel! Who do we have joining us today?" She had a very warm and inviting energy about her. She was a tall woman, too. She stood about six feet easily. She had the slim build of a runway model, long red hair, blue eyes, wore reading glasses, and she may have been in her late twenties. Uncle Kobe shook her hand and told Chase to introduce himself. "My name is Chase," he said, as he tried to match the smile that she was showcasing on her face. "Well, nice to meet you, Chase," she replied.

After a brief chat with Uncle Kobe, she instructed Chase to take his belongings into the classroom. Before he walked in, Uncle Kobe grabbed him and said, "Now remember, if you have a good day, I'll take you to the zoo next weekend. I'll even buy you a candy bar." Chase smiled even harder, nodded his head, and hugged him goodbye. Mrs. Sandel followed Chase into the classroom and closed the door behind her.

He looked around the room and waited to be told where to sit. His light, brown eyes scanned the room as he held on tightly to his toy. He had taken it out of his backpack while he and Uncle Kobe were greeting the teachers. "I'll hold on to that until playtime," Mrs. Sandel said, holding her hand out to receive the action figure from Chase. There were different sections in the classroom for the students. Each section had a number and a letter that represented their last name. Mrs. Sandel motioned for Chase to sit at the table that had the orange box on top of it.

There were two girls and two boys per table. As he sat down, only one of the students, Jessica, spoke to him. The other two turned their heads away and ignored him as if he wasn't there. Jessica introduced herself and tried to get the others to greet Chase as well. Her attempt failed, but that still didn't stop her. "Hi, I'm Jessica. What's your name?" she asked. Chase looked at her and repeated his name. He felt a little out of place. The size of the classroom was bigger than what he was used to in pre-school and being at home with Uncle Kobe. Jessica could tell that he was nervous, so she tried her best to cheer him up. "It's okay, I'll be your friend, Chase," she said, giving him a pat on the back. Her pretty smile and long ponytails matched the glow of her smooth, caramel colored skin. She had a matching bow in her head that was the same color as her blue skirt.

Her accent could be heard in her voice; she was the daughter of Barbadian immigrants. Jessica was a friendly, yet confident little girl. The class had gotten settled, and it was time to assign lockers to the students. Each one had been instructed to have a locker buddy, which meant that they would have to share the same space with a fellow student. Chase wasn't too thrilled about the idea, because he was used to having everything all to himself. Other than the few cousins that would come over for sleepovers every now and then, Chase had always been in his own domain. He was the only child in the house because Uncle Kobe didn't have any children of his own.

The teacher assigned the students their partners. One by one, she started pairing two at a time. When it was time for Chase to have his partner chosen, there was only one left. A little, brown-haired, white kid named Jake. He had pale, white skin, and a piercing look of terror in his dark, brown eyes. As Chase went to put his things into the locker,

Jake immediately stopped him. "No, you put your stuff at the bottom, darkie!" he said, as he grabbed his belongings and placed them on the top portion of the locker. Chase looked hurt and confused. He had no idea why the students in the classroom were being so mean and rude to him. Aside from Jessica, he felt as if he had stepped into uncharted territory.

When the class was settled, the students returned to their tables. Jake had his eyes on Chase the whole time. As Jake walked behind him, he put his foot in front of Chase and made him fall to the ground. The classroom rumbled with laughter, with the children pointing their fingers and mocking the way he had fallen. Chase looked up and saw the sinister grin on Jake's face. He couldn't believe that he had been embarrassed and humiliated in front of everyone. He didn't know what to do. He had never experienced bullying before, and even worse, Mrs. Sandel was nowhere to be found. She had stepped outside of the classroom briefly to help another teacher with a new curriculum.

With his fists balled, Chase stood up and confronted Jake. "I'm gonna tell the teacher on you when she comes back!" he said, with a burst of anger in his tone. Jake looked down at Chase's hands and knew that he meant business. He couldn't say much, because Mrs. Sandel had just stepped back into the classroom. "What are you two doing?" she asked. Jake wrapped his arms around Chase and hugged him. "Why Jake, that was very nice of you. I see you're already starting to make new friends," she said, with a smile on her face.

He knew what he was doing. The warm embrace was just a cover up for what his true intentions were. As Mrs. Sandel walked away, Jake whispered into Chase's ear. "You'd better stay out of my way, darkie!" Those words stuck with him for the remainder of the day. Jake walked back to his table where he was greeted with laughs and fist bumps from his table mates. It was rather odd because he was the only white kid at the table. There was one Mexican boy, and two other light-skinned girls.

Chase brushed it off and sat down beside Jessica. His feelings were hurt, but he refused to give Jake the satisfaction of letting him see it. He began to smile a little while complimenting Jessica's hair. "I like your hair," he said, pointing to her ponytails. "Thank you," Jessica replied. "Who did your hair like that?" she asked, gently tugging at one of Chase's dreadlocks. Before he could answer, the teacher intervened. "Remember one of our class rules, Jessica. Always keep our hands to ourselves."

She looked away and placed her hands into her lap. Chase didn't understand what was going on. It couldn't have been that bad. Jake had just given him a phony hug not less than a minute ago. Maybe those rules applied to certain other students, he thought. He liked the fact that Jessica would talk to him. How she acted towards Chase made him feel safe and secure. Besides, her smile, at least for the moment, could ease whatever tension he was dealing with.

A few hours had passed, and Chase hadn't managed

to make any new friends. However, he did participate in a few of the classroom activities that were presented by the teacher. There were alphabet, coloring, and number identifying exercises that had taken place. By the end of the activities, he had established himself as one of the smartest kids in the classroom. Jake, on the other hand, could barely identify the letters of the alphabet. He would always end up stopping at the letter "R." Maybe that was why he was so aggressive.

The children were all told to line up in a single file line. It was time to go outside for playtime. That was music to Chase's ears. He was anxious to go to the playground and swing on the monkey bars. "Here you go, Chase," said Mrs. Sandel, as she gave him his toy action figure that he had brought into the classroom earlier. He smiled and thanked her as he clutched his toy tightly. All at once, the students headed outside to get some much- needed recess. The sun was shining, and the temperature had cooled enough to where the teachers didn't have to worry about one of the children passing out.

When the students made it to the playground, they broke off into different groups and began to play with each other. As they leaped and jumped with joy, one of the little girls, Josie, decided to start a game of "Hide and Seek" with the other kids. They all had to line up and wait to be chosen by one of the team captains. Josie was the captain of her squad, and Jake was the captain of his. The students lined up and waited anxiously to be selected by one of the captains. One by one, the two chose their teammates. Only two people were left, Jessica and Chase.

"You gotta say you're not his friend anymore if you wanna play," said Josie, with her arms folded. She had one spot left, and clearly wasn't interested in choosing Chase for whatever reason. Jessica and Chase looked at each other with what seemed like a long stare. She really wanted to participate but didn't want to denounce her new friendship. "He's too short and too dark," Jake said as he pointed and laughed at Chase's skin complexion. Chase dropped his head and started playing with his action figure.

"Well, you wanna play or not?" Josie asked. She was becoming impatient and was anxious to play like all the other kids. To Chase's surprise, Jessica chose the latter and said something that he wasn't expecting her to say. "Yea, let's play. Besides, I think he may even have the cooties! He's too short and ugly" she said, as she ran over to join Josie's team. "That's right, darkie," Jake said, as he continued to laugh at the tears that had begun to stream down Chase's face.

Jessica waited until everyone ran off before joining them. It bothered her to see Chase crying. As she walked away, she slowly turned around and whispered to him. "I'm sorry," she said as she shrugged her shoulders and went to join her team. The hurt that Chase was feeling immediately turned into anger. He didn't want an apology. He wanted to play with the other kids like a normal child should. He rolled his eyes and turned his back as he tried to wipe away his tears. The teasing, name calling, and finger pointing had run its course. He walked over to the monkey bars, stood in front of the first set, and slammed his action figure into them.

The pieces splattered everywhere, and nothing other than the head could be identifiable. All alone, he sat down and put his face into his hands. The tears started to flow effortlessly as he tried to process what had just transpired. Mrs. Sandel had been watching the situation unfold for quite some time. She saw that the students had formed teams to play a game but knew something wasn't right when she saw that Chase had yet to be selected for one of them. She also was shocked at the strength he had possessed. The toy that he had thrown and broken was a collector's item, which meant that it was specially made with a tougher material than most.

Seeing that he was not doing okay, she ran over to check on him. "What's wrong, Chase?" she asked, being sympathetic to the situation. He lifted his head with tears in his eyes and shouted, "Everybody hates me!" Mrs. Sandel quickly grabbed Chase and hugged him. He sobbed even louder as he was being comforted. "Just breathe for me, Chase. Try to relax for me," she said. Hugging him was one thing but calming him down would be another. "I just wanna go home," he said, as he looked around to see if anyone was watching him. No one was around. It was just him and his teacher. The other kids were laughing and playing. He could even see that Jessica had found a nice hiding spot to keep her away from the kids on the opposite team.

Mrs. Sandel helped Chase dust himself off and held his hand as they walked over to the shaded area of the playground. She grabbed her purse and pulled out a green and orange lollipop. "Here, maybe this will cheer you up," she said, handing it to Chase. He nibbled and licked on it quietly, as he sat and watched the other kids have the time of their lives. Although she had given him the lollipop, Mrs. Sandel could see that Chase was still visibly upset. She looked over at him and said, "I'm about to make a phone call for you." He continued eating his lollipop and had almost forgotten about what had taken place. Mrs. Sandel sat and talked with Chase for a little while. The more he expressed himself, she realized that he was an incredibly special student.

Before they could finish, a tall, broad, light-skinned man appeared and hovered over Chase. He had a slightly deep voice, stood about six feet and two inches, brown eyes, and a nicely trimmed goatee. "Hey, little man, what's up?" he asked. "Uncle Kobe!!!" Chase shouted, as he jumped up and ran into his arms. There were only 30 minutes left in the day before the students would have to return to the classroom to prepare for departure. Seeing that Chase was having a tough first day of school, his teacher had decided to give his uncle a call. She figured it would brighten his day just a little, and it did.

She gave Uncle Kobe permission to go into the classroom to retrieve Chase's items. When he returned, he grabbed Chase's hand and began walking towards the school exit. "Thank you for my lollipop, Mrs. Sandel!" Chase shouted, as he was disappearing into the school's perimeter. Mrs. Sandel just smiled and waved goodbye. Chase was relieved that his nightmare was over. Seeing Uncle Kobe made him feel as if the world had stopped for a second. He didn't have to deal with mean, snotty kids anymore…at least not for the rest of the day.

They made it to the car and Uncle Kobe fastened Chase's seatbelt. As they headed home, Chase was abnormally quiet. Uncle Kobe decided to break the ice a little. "So, did you have fun today?" he asked, anticipating a response from his nephew. Chase looked out of the window and responded, "Not really." Uncle Kobe didn't get a bad report from the teacher, which made him ponder a little. "Did you make any friends today, man?" Uncle Kobe asked. Chase shook his head no and continued to stare out of the window. Before Uncle Kobe could ask another question, Chase interjected with one of his own. "Uncle Kobe, why am I ugly? What's a darkie?" Uncle Kobe slowed the car down and pulled over immediately. He removed Chase from the vehicle and asked him to repeat the question again.

"Who the hell called you a darkie?" Uncle Kobe asked, becoming irate about the things being told to him. "The girls said I was too short, too. They all made fun of me. Why don't I have your skin?" Chase asked questions while Uncle

Kobe tried to take in the information that was being given to him. He had no idea that Chase's first day of school would consist of him being teased about his height, and skin color. Uncle Kobe looked at Chase and told him to never worry about what people had to say about him. He assured him that his skin complexion was a gift from God and the sun. "Your pride and identity are within your features and your hair. Never forget that, man!" Uncle Kobe stated, as he helped Chase back into the car.

"So, everything they said about me wasn't true, Uncle Kobe?" Chase asked. "Well, they had one thing correct, man," Uncle Kobe replied. He had a grin on his face but wouldn't say what it was. Of all the things he had mentioned to Uncle Kobe, he couldn't pinpoint what he could've said that would be funny to him. "You are short, but don't worry about your height. I was short like you as a kid, too, man. We are late bloomers. You'll be fine," Uncle Kobe said, as he watched Chase in his rearview mirror. He told him to always embrace who he was and to appreciate the things that made him different from everybody else.

"Never be afraid to talk to me. I'm here for you no matter what, little man," Uncle Kobe said, as they were approaching the driveway to his house. As they pulled in, Uncle Kobe continued lecturing him about the importance of self-confidence and awareness. As he talked, Chase could see Dory leaning against the mailbox, smoking her cigarette. She had given him a very unpleasant look as they entered the driveway. "From now on, I'm gonna call you Tiu-Loo,"

Uncle Kobe said. "What kind of name is that?" Chase asked.

Uncle Kobe explained to him that when he was a young boy, he would have similar battles. Kids thought he was too little, but he was always one of the strongest kids in the neighborhood. He was short, but was still fast, quick, and swift. One of the local hustlers in the neighborhood, Daegus, ended up giving Uncle Kobe the name. "Now, I'm passing it down to you," Uncle Kobe said as he parked the car. Chase didn't know what to say, but after hearing the story, he thought it had a nice ring to it. "Is there anything else you would like to discuss with me?" Uncle Kobe asked. Chase looked out of the back window and could still see Dory watching him. "Just one more thing…. HER, Uncle Kobe!" Chase said, while pointing in her direction. Uncle Kobe was not too thrilled about the things that Chase was saying about his beloved Dory.

Chapter 2: Big Chief

He had tossed and turned in his bed for most of the night. He wondered if the lady in his dreams with the long, blue dress, and neatly braided dreadlocks could've been his mother. He would wake up periodically to look at the engraved bracelet that was given to him for his thirteenth birthday. It was gold plated, and had his initials with the caption, "Mommy's Miracle" etched into it. It was the final gift that his uncle had given him after a spectacular birthday weekend. His mother, Lameenah, had certain gifts that she'd hand made for him before she passed away.

Sleep wasn't going to find him anytime soon, so he decided to go into the kitchen to drink some lemonade and eat a slice of pizza. Uncle Kobe was a great cook, but it seemed as if his lemonade had been homebrewed by the Gods themselves. Tiu-Loo consumed the pizza and headed over to the couch to watch television. It was two o'clock in the morning and Uncle Kobe was knocked out. The snow had finally started to hit the ground, and Christmas had come and gone within that week. Tiu-Loo scanned through the channels before coming to a halt on one of his favorite comedy shows.

Unable to hold his composure from the entertainment, his loud laughter easily woke his uncle up from his sleep.

An extremely light sleeper, Uncle Kobe was one of those guys who probably could really hear a pin drop if it did. As he took his last sip of lemonade, Uncle Kobe walked into the living room to see what was going on. "What's up, man? Why are you up so late?" he asked, as he broke into a long stretch. "I just couldn't sleep. I keep having these weird dreams," Tiu-Loo replied, as he turned the volume down on the television. Uncle Kobe sat on the other end of the couch and asked Tiu-Loo about the dream.

After Tiu-Loo went over the details of the dream, Uncle Kobe broke out into a hysterical laugh. "Yea, that wasn't your mother. The hair? Maybe. But she definitely wouldn't have had a blue dress on. She loved her earth-toned and basic pastel colors!" he said, as he watched the show that Tiu-Loo had started. Still curious, he questioned his uncle. "What really happened to my mother?" he asked, with a serious look on his face. Uncle Kobe grabbed the remote control, turned the television off, and sat up to face Tiu-Loo. They had never really discussed his mother in that manner. All he knew was that she was free-spirited, an herbalist, and that she could lay her hair into her lap if she wanted to, because it was that long.

He slowly started explaining to Tiu-Loo that his mother had a very high-risk pregnancy. She was doing well until she was about six months pregnant. After his father was deported, stress and severe depression had begun to creep up on her. She became extremely ill, and when it was time to give birth to Tiu-Loo, she had to make a choice between her life and his. At that very moment, his mother knew that she had fulfilled her purpose in life. Without a second guess, she opted to save the life of her unborn son. Knowing that she probably wouldn't make it, she and Uncle Kobe agreed that he would be Tiu-Loo's legal guardian.

His eyes watered and his mouth dropped, as he listened to Uncle Kobe go into the vivid details of the accounts that had taken place leading up to his mother's untimely passing. He was saddened about what had taken place but was inspired at the same time. "I don't know what to say. She sacrificed so much, and I never got the chance to meet her," said Tiu-Loo has he wiped the one tear that had successfully made it down his face. He wanted to blame himself, but Uncle Kobe assured him that there was nothing that anyone could do. He explained to him that although unfortunate, death is a natural part of life.

It's as if Tiu-Loo's mother could foresee the future. She had made a few items for him that she had instructed Uncle Kobe to give him at a certain point in his life. The bracelet was a reminder of his mother's unconditional love for him, as well as his introduction into manhood. By the tradition of his family, once a young man reached the age of thirteen, he had officially started his journey of becoming a man. The information that Tiu-Loo was receiving would prove to be vital for him later in his life.

After a few laughs and cries, Uncle Kobe went back into his bedroom. With everything that had been shared with him, Tiu-Loo had definitely gone into a different headspace. Surely his mother could have chosen her life over his own, but she unselfishly made a decision that was obviously bigger than her. At that moment, he had developed an insurmountable amount of respect and love for his mother. One that he would forever hold near and dear to his heart.

In the living room, on top of one of Uncle Kobe's bookshelves, stood an old photo album. As a kid, Tiu-Loo had never paid any attention to it. He grabbed the album and made his way back to the couch. He snickered and almost fell off the couch when he saw an old picture of Uncle Kobe with an afro. That was a hilarious site for him to see, indeed. As he continued to flip through the photos, one picture immediately caught his attention. There was a woman with long dreadlocks, a huge smile, and wearing a nicely fitted sundress. Beside her stood a tall, dark-skinned man with a broad nose, full lips, and a necklace with African seashells on it. The shells looked remarkably familiar; Uncle Kobe kept a similar necklace in his car that hung from his rearview mirror.

Without a shadow of a doubt, Tiu-Loo knew that the two individuals in the picture were his mother and his father. He shared the same smile and facial features as his mother, while his skin tone came directly from his father. His mother seemed to be full of love and joy in the photo. His father had his arms around her waist and seemed to look at her with a playful smirk on his face. He believed that his parents were genuinely happy together, and for uncontrollable reasons, unfortunate circumstances would eventually cause them to have their lives separated.

He took the picture out of the photo album and ran into his uncle's bedroom. "Hey Uncle Kobe, can you get this picture blown up, so that I can frame it?" he asked. Uncle Kobe was slowly fading back to sleep and softly replied, "Sure thing, man. Now go get some sleep." Tiu-Loo sat the picture on his uncle's nightstand and walked out. He was relieved, because all the questions that he had pertaining to his parents were answered. His uncle was very good and patient about accurately explaining things to him. That was one trait that Tiu-Loo absolutely loved about Uncle Kobe. He went to bed and slept peacefully through the night.

Another week had gone by, and it was time to get ready for the start of the new semester. Now an eighth grader, Tiu-Loo had learned how to be more of a recluse in school. After successfully completing elementary school, he was promoted and attended the middle school of the same name, Carver Middle. This unfortunately meant that some of the same students who had teased and picked at him, would migrate over to the new school as well. Tiu-Loo did all he could to keep himself busy and from being distracted by others. He participated in after school activities and would take up extra credit assignments whenever he could.

Torment would still make its way to him at times, however. He would get the occasional "go back to Africa," or "hello, Mister Darkness" jokes from time to time. Some of the jokes were odd to him, because most of them would come from other black students. He would just brush it off and continue with his day. He didn't care what any of the other students said to him, as long as they didn't touch him. Before the start of his seventh-grade year, Uncle Kobe decided to train Tiu-Loo. They would run, lift light weights, and spar with each other by doing boxing rounds. He single-handedly helped to build Tiu-Loo's confidence.

Before it was all said and done, Tiu-Loo had put on twelve pounds of muscle, gained insane endurance, his confidence was through the roof, and most importantly, he knew how to fight. Uncle Kobe would always break down the rules of conflict and engagement to Tiu-Loo. "Remember, a real man doesn't start things. He ends them!" Uncle Kobe would remind Tiu-Loo of this quote each day after every sparring session. Some of the things the kids would say still hurt him, but he was ready to fight if he felt threatened or needed to defend himself. Fortunately, they kept it at only joking and teasing.

Early one morning, during the start of his eighth-grade year, Tiu-Loo was getting his schedule prepared. He was in the school gymnasium with many other students awaiting the arrival of the school principal and guidance counselor. The final classes and teachers were to be assigned, so that the students could officially begin the school year. As he sat alone on the opposite side of the bleachers, a young man walked into the gym holding a folder in his hand. Tiu-Loo was curious to know what he was doing. The guy was a new student; he had never seen him at school before.

The young man had on a designer t-shirt with a pair of shoes and a backpack to match. He was tall, had a slim build, a light-brown skin tone, and a neat haircut with waves in his head. He seemed to draw attention effortlessly when he walked into any room. As he entered the gym, the young ladies started to blush and whisper as they marveled at his good looks. "Girl, he's fine as hell!" one of the young ladies said, as a few of her other friends nodded in agreement. The young man paid no attention. Some of the other guys motioned for him to come sit with them, but instead, he went over to the opposite side of the bleachers and sat in the same area as Tiu-Loo.

Tiu-Loo was stunned. The young man would've easily blended in with the other popular kids if he had sat with them. Apparently being popular didn't matter to him. Like Tiu-Loo, he was trying to get his schedule together. After a few silent minutes, he turned to ask Tiu-Loo a question. "Hey boy-boy, would you happen to know where Mr. Finch's class is?" Tiu-Loo tried to comprehend the name that the young man had referred to him as. "Boy what?" he asked, with a look of uncertainty on his face. The young man laughed as he saw how off- center Tiu-Loo looked. "Boy-boy. It's just an expression that we use in New York. I'm from Harlem," the young man explained.

"That's what's up," said Tiu-Loo. The young man introduced himself as he extended his hand. "I'm Kato, by the way," he said. "I'm Chase, but everyone calls me Tiu-Loo," he replied. "Well Tiu-Loo it is, boy-boy," Kato said, as he firmly shook Tiu-Loo's hand. Tiu-Loo asked Kato to pass him the folder so that he could help him with his schedule. "Mr. Finch is the Physical Education teacher. It looks like you and I will be taking his class together during fourth period," Tiu-Loo explained. "Sounds like a bet," Kato replied.

Kato and his mother had moved down south once she was promoted at her job. She had been working for a company that manufactured computers for about ten years. As the two continued to converse and become acquainted, the other students were in disbelief. Other than the school janitor, and a few of the teachers, no one really said much to Tiu-Loo other than the daily insults and character slandering. You would've thought a ghost had appeared by the way they were looking at them.

The principal was taking too long, and Tiu-Loo really needed to go to the restroom. The liter of bottled water he had consumed that morning had finally reached his bladder. "I'll be back," he said to Kato, as he started a fast-paced walk out of the gym. Another student waited a few seconds and followed behind him in the same direction. Tiu-Loo immediately relieved himself as soon as he made it to the restroom. He almost thought he would be too late. He exhaled with relief. "Woo, that was close!" he said to himself, as he was finishing up. He zipped his pants and proceeded to wash his hands in the sink.

Before he could finish washing his hands, the door swung open with force. Three boys walked in and grabbed Tiu-Loo. "Hey darkie, you been staying in the jungle lately?" one of the boys asked. He instantly recognized the voice. It was Jake! He had been watching Tiu-Loo all morning long. He made sure he didn't see him while they were in the gymnasium. He had transferred to another school his seventh-grade year to live with his father. Evidently, that didn't work out, because here he was yet again torturing Tiu-Loo. "The hell ya'll doin? Let me go!" Tiu-Loo yelled. Jake pulled a big bottle of soda from his backpack. The boys held Tiu-Loo tighter. They forced him to the ground, as Jake stood over him.

"I see the gorilla hasn't learned his lesson," he said, as he unscrewed the top from the bottle. He wasted no time. He poured the soda all over Tiu-Loo's hair. The cold soda made him shiver as it soaked and stained his new shirt. He yelled and tried to get free, but the weight of one of the heavier boys kept him on the ground. One of his arms were pinned under him, while the other was being held by another assailant. Jake pulled a pair of scissors from his pocket and kneeled in front of Tiu-Loo.

"Don't you touch my damn hair!" Tiu-Loo shouted, with obvious rage in his voice. "I think it's time for a makeover. What do you guys think?" he asked, as he smirked at the two boys. "Hell yea! Do that shit!" the bigger boy said. "I think I'll cut this one," Jake said, as he grabbed one of the longer dreadlocks that were on Tiu-Loo's head. He stopped at about half the length of the loc and cut it. Tiu-Loo squirmed and moved his body as much as he could, but the attempt was useless. He was simply overpowered. "Think I'll keep this for decoration," said Jake. He took the loc and placed it in his pocket. Agony and defeat were all that Tiu-Loo could feel at that moment.

His dreadlocks had grown a little past his shoulders over the years. They meant a lot to him. He absolutely cherished them! To add insult to injury, the smaller boy snatched Tiu-Loo's bracelet from his wrist. "I'll take that!" he uttered. It was his first time wearing it to school, and it was the bracelet that his mother had made for him. The three boys ran out of the bathroom and went back into the gym as if nothing had happened. They sat on the bleachers and mingled with the rest of the students.

Tiu-Loo sat on the restroom floor. He couldn't believe what had just taken place. Whatever pride and dignity he thought he had was taken away in an instant. He started crying and beating his hand on the restroom stall. His feelings were hurt immensely. The soda being poured on him was tolerable, but the cutting of his hair and theft of his bracelet was unacceptable. He had been attacked, and with his emotions running high, there was no way he could let that slide. He gathered himself, stood up, and looked in the mirror. He remembered what his uncle had taught him. "A real man doesn't start things. He ends them!"

He tied his shoes up, took off his soaked shirt, and

headed towards the gym. Feeling good about what they had done, the boys started bragging to the other students about the events that had just taken place. Claudia, an uppity and popular white girl, thought that the story was hilarious. "So, the monkey is back in the jungle after all," she said, as she laughed with Jake and the other two boys. "You might like this," the smaller boy replied, as he pulled out the bracelet that he had snatched from Tiu-Loo's wrist. "It is pretty," Claudia said, as she attempted to try it on.

Tiu-Loo finally made it to the gym. The students were so busy interacting with each other, that they didn't see him walking in. Everyone was pre-occupied except for Kato. He could see the balled-up fists, heavy breathing, and the look of death in Tiu-Loo's eyes. He had quickly realized that something bad had happened during Tiu-Loo's trip to the restroom. The soda was still dripping from Tiu-Loo's hair. Kato had no idea what was going on, but he knew that Tiu-Loo was visibly upset.

He scanned the gym carefully as he located his target. There they were. Jake and his buddies were giggling and having a good ole time on the third row of the bleachers. Tiu-Loo quickly ran over to the area where Jake was sitting. He cleared the first two rows of bleachers in no time. Before anyone could react, Tiu-Loo had punched Jake with a fierce right hand to the face. He had landed a few more punches before anyone had realized what was happening. He grabbed Jake and dragged him down the bleacher steps onto the gym floor, where he continued to pulverize him.

Jake was getting hit so hard, that he was starting to black out.

Claudia and the rest of the students crowded around the fight in disbelief. They had never seen anyone so angry and upset. The last thing anyone thought was that Tiu-Loo would ever get into a physical altercation with anyone, especially not with the likes of Jake. They thought wrong. The quiet one who had been getting teased and somewhat bullied was getting the absolute best of Jake.

Realizing that their comrade was in grave danger, the two boys who had assisted with the assault in the restroom rushed to Jake's aid. They tackled Tiu-Loo to the ground and began punching him. The students all screamed and shouted in unison, as they seemed to side with the boys who were jumping him. It was a clear indication that no one was going to help Tiu-Loo. It wasn't long before a fist met the side of the bigger boy's face and sent him flying across the floor. It had come from out of nowhere.

Kato had watched the whole scene unfold, and although he had just met Tiu-Loo, he was not going to sit back and let him get jumped. Once he saw the other two boys joining in, he hurried over and punched the biggest one. The boy struggled to gain his composure, as the punch that had landed was devastating. Claudia yelled out, "Hey, just let them fight. This has nothing to do with you!" "Ain't no one-on-ones BITCH!" Kato shouted back, daring the bigger boy to jump in again. The phrase was taught to him by one of his cousins from Chicago. It simply implied that if one of us fight, then we all fight. That was the code, and that was the way. What was understood didn't have to be explained at all.

After getting hit with such power, the bigger boy opted to stay out of the fight. Jake was still on the ground with his eye almost swollen completely shut. The only person left was the smaller boy. Tiu-Loo punched him a few times and then in one motion, picked him up and slammed him hard to the ground. The force was so great that you could hear one of his ribs cracking. As the bigger boy started to retreat through the crowd, Tiu-Loo and Kato chased him down. Kato stuck his foot out making him trip and stumble to the ground. He ran over and put him in a choke hold. "You sat on top of me and let him cut my hair!" Tiu-Loo said, as he wailed away at him with punches to the face and body.

He continued to punch until the school security guard finally intervened. He grabbed Tiu-Loo and tried to restrain him, but he was too antsy and upset. "I'm sick of this shit!" Tiu-Loo shouted, as the security guard and one of the faculty members carried him away. The school principal, Mr. Bolden, had finally made it to the gym. The fight was more serious than he had imagined. He approached Kato and told him to come to his office as well. The three boys looked like they had been beaten by grown men. Jake's left eye was now swollen shut, the smaller boy had a broken rib, and the bigger boy had a busted lip and swollen face. The students in the gym were left completely dumbstruck.

Once they arrived in the principal's office, he sat them both down and attempted to question them. The security guard and another faculty member had escorted Jake and his friends down as well. Tiu-Loo was still upset, his body trembled as he wanted to fight Jake again when he saw his face in the same room as him. "What happened to your shirt?" Mr. Bolden asked. "Why don't you ask him," Tiu-Loo replied, staring directly at Jake. "Well Jake, what happened to his shirt?" he asked, as he folded his arms waiting for an explanation.

Before Jake could explain what happened, Tiu-Loo interrupted him. He broke down the situation in its entirety to Mr. Bolden. He explained how Jake had been a bully and nuisance to him since the first day of kindergarten. He continued to express similar situations he had endured by the same students even after he had transitioned over to middle school. As he continued, he was overcome with emotion. "And then they held me down while Jake cut my hair," he cried, as Mr. Bolden immediately reached out to embrace him. There wasn't a dry eye in the principal's office. Hearing Tiu-Loo tell his story with such passion had the faculty in tears as well. Only Kato sat with a straight face, and no emotion. He felt bad for Tiu-Loo, but he also admired his courage. He was glad that he had helped him fight and would do it again if he had to.

"You can check in his pockets right now. You'll find one of my dreadlocks," Tiu-Loo said, as he insisted that Jake had placed it there. The security officer checked his pockets, and low and behold, Tiu-Loo's hair was exactly where he said it would be. He also got his bracelet back that the boys had taken as well. Mr. Bolden was at a loss for words. He wondered how such a bright kid could harbor that much hurt and pain. "Here boy-boy, put this on," Kato said, as he took off his shirt. He had another t-shirt under his original one. He was tired of seeing Tiu-Loo without one, so he offered his. Tiu-Loo thanked him and quickly put the shirt on.

"I'm expelling all of you. Especially you, Todd!" Mr. Bolden assured. Todd, the bigger boy, was on his second term in the eighth grade. His dad was a red-neck, confederate flag wielding alcoholic. He had missed many days the year before, and when he did come to school, he always got into trouble. "What was your involvement in this?" Mr. Bolden asked, as he directed his attention to Richard, the smaller boy. Mostly a quiet student, he was a Mexican kid, who loved to skateboard from time to time. His flaw was his loyalty to his best friend, Jake. They had been friends since head start. Whatever Jake told him to do, he would just go along with it. He always possessed the characteristics of a follower.

After making them all apologize to Tiu-Loo, Mr. Bolden called their parents, and had them dismissed. Tiu-Loo knew that his hair would grow back, but he was relieved and a bit content once he placed the bracelet back on his wrist. It was sentimental and irreplaceable. Furthermore, it was the only direct link he had that could be attached to his mother. Mr. Bolden walked back into his office and spoke with the young men. "Unfortunately, I'm going to have to suspend you two as well, but only for three days," he said, as he winked at them. Of course, he had to yield some type of punishment for the rumble that had occurred.

They didn't mind. It was considered a slap on the wrist to them. Mr. Bolden admired and respected the fact that Kato had defended Tiu-Loo while he was being jumped. Besides, the two young man technically didn't start the fight. The fight caused Tiu-Loo to develop an appetite. Mr. Bolden had a box of donuts on his desk, and Tiu-Loo had been looking at them for a while now. After watching him carefully, Mr. Bolden grabbed a few napkins and offered a couple to Kato and Tiu-Loo. The young men sat back and ate the donuts, as Mr. Bolden made his way to the intercom to make an announcement.

"Alright, students. Let's have a productive day. If you have your class schedules finalized, report to them now," he announced. As the students were released from the gymnasium, the first thing they did was make a trip to the principal's office. Even if their class wasn't on that path, that still didn't stop them from seeing what had happened with Tiu-Loo, and the new kid. They passed by in flocks, taking a peep through the see-through glass of Mr. Bolden's office. Many of the girls waved at the young men as they smiled and walked by. "That new boy got hands," one of the girls said, as she and her friend smiled and waved at Kato.

Uncle Kobe had already been informed about the fight that Tiu-Loo was involved in. After the principal explained to him how everything started, his mind was put at ease. He was proud of his nephew and was glad that he had stood up for himself. He stuck to his morals and values, while still exhibiting the spirit of a warrior. He executed his actions in the way that Uncle Kobe taught him, and for that, Tiu-Loo had proven that he had been listening and learning. Kato's mother was only shocked because the semester hadn't even started yet. She was used to him getting into a few fights here and there.

A lot of the kids where he grew up would be jealous of him, because of his style, and the clothes he would wear. They would mistake him as being a "pretty boy" but when they would try to fight him, his style wasn't pretty at all. He never lost a fight and was still a very humble young man. It wasn't his fault that his mother could afford nice things for him. He wore his clothes, went to school, and would mind his own business.

The young men waved at the girls as they walked by. Some of the guys even stood in the window while giving them praise on what they had done. Claudia stopped by the office and asked if she could hand something over to Tiu-Loo. Mr. Bolden told her it was fine, as long as Tiu-Loo was okay with it. She walked in and handed a folded sheet of paper over to him. He didn't know what to think. *Why was she giving me anything?* He wondered. She thanked Mr. Bolden and walked out of the office.

"I'm not about to read this," Tiu-Loo said, as he passed the folded paper to Kato. Kato opened the letter and started laughing. "Looks like you got a crush, boy-boy," he said, as he continued to read the letter. "What? Let me see that," Tiu Loo replied, as he leaned over to read along. It was true. While laughing at and making fun of Tiu-Loo with Jake and his friends, she was secretly infatuated with Tiu-Loo. She had even left her phone number in the letter for Tiu-Loo to contact her. "I guess she has a little jungle fever for the jungle boy," Tiu-Loo said, as he and Kato continued to laugh with each other.

Although a little intrigued by what the letter said, Tiu-Loo didn't trust it. There's no way she could have felt any of those things that she had mentioned. "This is gonna be an interesting rest of the school year," said Kato, as he got up and prepared to leave. His mother had arrived to pick him up from school. "I'll see you in three days, boy-boy," he said, as he shook hands with Tiu-Loo. Before he walked out, Tiu-Loo stopped him. He balled the letter up and handed it over to him. "Throw this away for me," he said. Kato threw the paper in the trash can and headed outside to his mother.

Chapter 3: By Default

"I don't know, boy-boy. I think it may be more than a gas issue this time," said Kato, as he opened the door to help Tiu-Loo push his car to the side of the road. Uncle Kobe had helped Tiu-Loo buy a vehicle over the summer, so that he wouldn't have to walk to school during his senior year. He and Kato had been driving for a few minutes after leaving a school football game, when his car abruptly stopped in the middle of the street. He tried to turn the keys in the ignition several times, but none of his attempts seemed to work. Luckily, he had insurance and roadside assistance. After making the phone call, he stood there with Kato and discussed the year's final activities.

"Did you see how Nicole was looking at you?" Kato asked. "Nah, she was looking at you, bro. I'm big ugly," said Tiu-Loo, as he looked away from Kato. "You play too much, boy-boy," said Kato, as the two began to laugh at each other. Tiu-Loo had gained a lot of respect since the brawl that had taken place years ago in middle school. He wasn't the short, scrawny, and timid little boy anymore. He had grown to be a rather handsome young man. He was nearly six feet tall, had a slim, built muscular frame, and his hair had now extended down close to the middle of his back. Although he was still self-conscious about his skin color, he had embraced himself, and had managed to become popular amongst his peers. The young ladies loved his hair. There weren't too many days that would pass by where one of them wouldn't ask to play in or touch it.

Nicole was one of the captains on the cheerleading squad. She met Tiu-Loo at the beginning of her freshman year in high school, and the two had been close ever since. There was a slight worry entering the senior school year because they both were planning to attend separate colleges that would be hundreds of miles away from each other. Anyone could see that there was obvious chemistry between the two, but Tiu-Loo would never make a move, and Nicole was too afraid of rejection. They would go to the movies on some weekends, and on many occasions, Tiu-Loo would sit between her legs as she oiled and massaged his scalp and dreadlocks. She had a noticeably confident walk. She had a positive attitude, and her hips would be noticed before you could see her face. Her five- foot frame came with curves, brown skin, almond-shaped eyes, and dimples in both cheeks. With all the attention she garnered because of her looks, she only appeared to have eyes for Tiu-Loo.

"Why don't you ask her to prom?" Kato asked. He had seen first-hand how the two were with one another and had personally grown tired of watching them play cat and mouse. "Man, hell no. And have people thinking we go together?" Tiu-Loo replied, as he looked at Kato. He cared about his friendship with Nicole but didn't want to give off the wrong impression by asking her to go to the prom with him. "Who cares what people think. You better man up, boy-boy, or I'll ask her for you. Do you have her number?" Kato asked, as he pulled his phone from his pockets. "Yea, I'll send it to you on a bullet," Tiu-Loo replied, with a slight grin on his face.

He promised Kato that he would ask her soon, once he felt the time was right. After several minutes of conversing, a man driving a tow truck pulled over to take a look at Tiu-Loo's car. The heavy-set man got in and turned the key. "How long has this check engine light been on?" he asked Tiu-Loo. "I don't know. A couple of months maybe," Tiu-Loo replied. The man got out of the car and lifted the hood. He grabbed a paper towel from his coveralls to check the oil level. When the dipstick came up dry, he knew exactly what the issue was.

"Yea, the motor's shot!" the man said. Tiu-Loo couldn't believe it. He asked the man how that could have been possible. "There was no oil in the car whatsoever. I'm surprised your car held up this long," the man replied. "Damn it! I forgot again." Tiu-Loo shouted. Uncle Kobe had explained to him that checking his oil regularly was just as important as putting gas in his car. Tiu-Loo took the loss and understood that it was his fault. His uncle had done his part with purchasing the vehicle, but it was his responsibility to maintain and take care of it.

The sun started going down, and he offered to take

Tiu-Loo and Kato home as he towed the car to the same destination. When they arrived, the man lowered the car, and dropped it in front of Tiu-Loo's house. Tiu-Loo thanked him and checked the mailbox. He had been waiting on acceptance letters from a few universities. A couple did reach out, but none of them were offering full scholarships just yet. He was an exceptional student. He took honors classes and mostly made As and Bs in them, but Calculus was giving him a run for his money. He couldn't manage to get higher than a C minus in the course, and that was preventing his GPA from being as high as he would've liked it to be. Also, the teacher, Coach David, was relentless. Your grade was your grade. He didn't believe in make-up work or extra credit. Tiu-Loo was aware of the battle he had on his hands.

"You might as well stay over tonight," Tiu-Loo said to Kato. "Oh, that was the plan anyway, boy-boy," Kato replied. He only lived a few blocks down from Tiu-Loo, but he didn't feel like walking home at that moment. They went inside and made their way to the kitchen. There were some leftovers in the refrigerator from the night before. Fried chicken, macaroni and cheese, loaded baked potatoes, and Uncle Kobe's homemade apple pie were waiting to meet their fate. "I'm about to smash, boy-boy," Kato said, as he prepared his plate and warmed it in the microwave. Kato was like another family member by now. His mother worked long hours at her job, so he would come by almost every day to hang with Tiu-Loo and partake in eating whatever food Uncle Kobe would prepare that day. Uncle Kobe didn't mind at all. He thought it was cool that Tiu-Loo had made a genuine friend who looked out for him.

The young men dove into their meal, barely taking a breath in between bites. Pushing Tiu-Loo's car had given them quite an appetite. As Kato got up to get another plate, Uncle Kobe walked in the door. It was a Friday night, and he had gone on a date with his co-worker. She was new to the city and wanted someone to show her around town. Quick to jump at the opportunity, Uncle Kobe volunteered his services. What was supposed to be an hour of sightseeing turned into almost four hours of a wonderful date.

He was perplexed when he saw Tiu-Loo's car sitting in front of the house; he would normally park it in the garage next to his. When he walked in, Tiu-Loo was rinsing his plate in the sink. "Hey man, what's wrong with your car?" Uncle Kobe asked, as he placed his keys on the dining room table. Tiu-Loo looked at him and replied, "Looks like I'll need a new motor." "What? Didn't I tell you to put oil in there just last week, Chase?" Uncle Kobe asked. Tiu-Loo hadn't heard that name in quite some time, but he knew that whenever Uncle Kobe called him by his government name, he was serious and not playing.

"Yes sir. It's my fault. I should've paid attention," Tiu-Loo replied. Uncle Kobe walked over to him and told him that he wouldn't be able to help him get another car. He had worked many hours to help save up the money to purchase the vehicle, and he didn't want to go through that process again. Tiu-Loo felt bad, because he knew the sacrifices that his uncle had made to do what he had done for him. He made a promise to be more mindful of his possessions and gave a sincere apology to Uncle Kobe. "Don't be sorry, be careful," Uncle Kobe replied. He hugged Tiu-Loo and walked to his bedroom. Before he closed his door, he made one last statement. "Oh yea, you're gonna have to walk to school for the rest of the year, too," Uncle Kobe said, as he shut his bedroom door.

Tiu-Loo had forgotten all about the schedule change. Uncle Kobe got up at five a.m. every morning to prepare for work. By 5:40, he was in the car and headed to his office. School didn't start until 7:45 for Tiu-Loo, which meant that he was still sound asleep when his uncle left home. Even if he wanted to, offering Tiu-Loo a ride to school would still be impossible. It finally hit Tiu-Loo how significant the loss of his car would be. He started to get upset. He wasn't mad at his uncle. It was the feeling of disappointment and not paying attention to detail that made him feel bad. Those were some of the lessons that Uncle Kobe would teach him while sparring and training together.

Watching his friend get down on himself, Kato tried to lift his spirits. "Hey, don't worry, boy-boy. We're only a mile and a half from the school. I'll mob with you," Kato said, as he threw his arm around Tiu-Loo's shoulder. "'Preciate that, man," Tiu-Loo replied. As they sat down to watch television, Tiu-Loo's cell phone started ringing. It was Nicole. She had finally made it home from the football game and wanted to see if Tiu-Loo felt like going out. "Let me take a rain check. I have some studying to do. I'll catch you later," he said, as he ended the phone call.

"Bro, what the hell are you doing?" Kato had been listening to him talk on the phone with Nicole and couldn't believe he had declined a night out with her. "What do you mean what am I doing?" Tiu-Loo asked. "See, you trippin', boy-boy." Kato explained. "It's a Friday night, she wants to go out with you alone, y'all obviously dig each other, and most importantly...it's Friday night. Hint...hint!" Kato said, as he looked at Tiu-Loo, hoping he would come to his senses. Tiu-Loo thought about it for a second. He did want to see her, but he had entirely too much on his mind. Between trying to ace his Calculus class and stressing about losing his car, he just wasn't in the right frame of mind.

"Alright, boy-boy, keep playing hard to get, and somebody else is gonna take her." Kato said, as he sat down to eat another slice of pie. "We're just friends, so I'm not trippin'," Tiu-Loo replied. Kato dismissed his claim and continued to eat his pie. He knew that Tiu-Loo liked Nicole, but for whatever reason, he was very hesitant on trying to pursue things with her. Not wanting to make his dear friend feel left out in the cold, Tiu-Loo sent her a text. "How about you tutor me. My Calculus class is kicking my ass," he texted. She immediately replied and said, "Sure thing, boo. Just meet me in the library after school."

They had the same teacher for Calculus, but during separate class periods. Tiu-Loo believed that Nicole could help him, because she had nothing but perfect scores in Coach David's class. "I still think you should go out with her tonight, but I'm gonna stay out of it," Kato said, while drinking a glass of lemonade. Tiu-Loo tried to ignore him, but deep down inside, he knew that Kato was right. If anyone knew what they were talking about, Kato had hit it on the nose.

Tiu-Loo would go to bed that night wondering whether his decision not to go out with Nicole was a bad one. Of all the girls who would try to throw themselves at him, he only wanted Nicole's attention. His trust with people in general was messed up. Although he had a good reputation at his school, he didn't care to make any new friends. He had grown accustomed to staying to himself, and only being in the company of those he really felt were sincere to him. Nicole was one of those people. He could talk to her about anything, she gave him great advice, and her smile alone would light his world up. There was no one like her, and he would soon tell her what he had been feeling.

The weekend had flown by, and it was time to get back to business. There were banners and posters decorating the hallways of the school. It had been over 25 years since the school's football team had achieved a winning season, and the weekend prior, they had won the playoff game that would send them to the divisional round. The players all huddled up, as they snapped photos with their fellow classmates. Even some of the teachers joined in the festivities while congratulating them on a job well done.

Once the parade was over, classes resumed as normal. Tiu-Loo dapped hands with Kato as they went in opposite directions. As he continued down the hall to his classroom, Nicole was walking out of the girl's bathroom. "Hey, shy guy. You trying to dodge me?" she asked, as she playfully put on a sad face. He told her that it wasn't like that. He just had a lot on his plate and wanted to handle things before it had become too overwhelming for him. Nicole understood him and respected his space. Although she liked him, she didn't want to crowd him or seem pushy.

"So, library after school?" Tiu-Loo asked while hugging Nicole. "Absolutely," she replied, with a huge smile on her face. They chatted for a minute until it was time for their classes to start. The first period of the day was unwelcoming for Tiu-Loo, because the dreaded Calculus class that Coach David taught was on the menu. He would go into the classroom, sit in the very back, take notes, and hope the teacher never called his name. However, like clockwork, Coach David would always find a way to include Tiu-Loo whenever a classroom activity presented itself. Tiu-Loo always felt as if his teacher was picking on him. It seemed as if he would find every opportunity that he could to make Tiu-Loo's day even more difficult.

This day would be no different from any of the rest. The teacher called students to the chalk board to manually solve the math problems he had assigned. On a normal day, Tiu-Loo would suck it up and participate. Today however, he just wasn't feeling it. Coach David had asked him several times to solve his math problem on the board, but he simply refused. After several attempts from the teacher, Tiu-Loo had finally lost his temper. "Man, I'm sick this shit! I'm out!" Tiu-Loo hopped from his desk and walked outside of the classroom. Everyone was quiet. Tiu-Loo had always kept to himself, but no one had ever witnessed him react the way that he did. Obviously a very uncharacteristic trait from Tiu-Loo, Coach David knew that something had to have been deeply affecting him.

Concerned, he went after Tiu-Loo to see what had been troubling him. When he walked outside, Tiu-Loo had his back against the wall, with his arms folded. Coach David cautiously approached him. "Hey, what was that all about? What's going on?" he asked Tiu-Loo. Before responding, Tiu-Loo relaxed himself. He let him know that while he was a great teacher, his class was difficult. Knowing and trying to comprehend the formulas of Calculus was just too frustrating. However, he knew that he needed the credit in order to graduate. Coach David sympathized with Tiu-Loo but explained to him that another outburst like that would not be tolerated. He advised him to seek a tutor. It was his own responsibility to ensure that his grades were up to par for graduation. "I'll let you cool down for a minute, but when you step into my classroom, be ready to learn," Coach David reiterated. A teacher for 30 years, he was a highly educated man from the Middle East. He was short in stature and wore signature glasses that kept his eyesight intact. Tiu-Loo's outburst wasn't the first he had seen in his career, but certainly the most surprising. Tiu-Loo apologized to his teacher without hesitation. He knew that he was wrong, and he also knew that a suspension or bad transcript could hurt his chances of attending the college of his choice. He was aware that he had to shift his focus, and he was determined to do so.

The day had come to an end, and it was time to meet Nicole in the library. Tiu-Loo was relieved when he saw that only a few students were occupying it. He walked in and met her in a corner where they would have more privacy. Nicole could sense that his energy was off. He wasn't laughing, he wasn't smiling, and he had this intense look on his face. "What's wrong? You look upset," she said, as they sat down at their table. He tried to blow it off as nothing, but Nicole knew him too well. They had been friends far too long for her to not realize when something was bothering him.

She didn't have to pry much before he ultimately gave in to her request. He was down about his car and hated the fact that his math class was getting the best of him. "Don't let that bother you, handsome. I got your back." Nicole said, as she put her hand on top of his. In an instant, he was calm. The world stopped around him. He was in sync with Nicole and what she was telling him. She knew that he was under a lot of stress and encouraged him not to be frustrated. Once he calmed down, she pulled her notes out to see what she could help him with.

Nicole simplified a few of the problems for him. After several examples, she let Tiu-Loo try a few on his own. For some reason, her method seemed to work. Whatever Coach David had been showing him just didn't resonate as well as Nicole's examples did. An hour had gone by and Tiu-Loo was running through the problems effortlessly. Nicole was right on time, because Coach David announced that the students would have four major quizzes before winter break, and he had no intentions of holding back. "See, there you go, boo!" Nicole said, as she rooted Tiu-Loo on. She was amazed at how quickly he had caught on, but then again, that was Tiu-Loo. "I just hope it's good enough to ace these quizzes," Tiu-Loo said, as he started to doubt himself. "Positive thoughts only, sir," Nicole said, while putting her notes away. She had to get ready for work and Kato had been outside of the library talking to one of the school cheerleaders, as he waited for Tiu-Loo. They walked to and from school together every day.

"Thank you so much," Tiu-Loo said, as he walked outside with Nicole. "Awww, there's my favorite couple," Kato said, as he went to greet them both. Nicole reminded Tiu-Loo that he didn't have to thank her for things that she had no problem helping him with. Yet, he was still a courteous and appreciative young man. Since losing his car over the weekend, he had started understanding what taking things for granted meant. As he hugged Nicole, she kissed him on the cheek and drove off. Kato looked away, hoping that they had exchanged a real kiss. "Nothing serious, bro. She always does that," Tiu-Loo said, as they started their walk home.

It had rained the night before, which caused many puddles to form in the streets and on the sidewalks. "I can't get my new shoes wet, boy-boy," Kato said, as he tiptoed around the small puddles they would encounter. "Man, you better use your legs and jump over them," Tiu-Loo replied, as he had already started the process. One by one, Tiu-Loo jumped the long puddles with single bound leaps. "Show off!" Kato joked, as he realized that Tiu-Loo had left him several yards behind.

Tiu-Loo continued what he was doing, until a blue car with lightly tinted windows pulled up next to him. The car was creeping at first, which alerted Kato. He immediately caught up with him to see who the person in the vehicle was. Finally coming to a complete stop, the passenger window slowly came down. "Hey Mr. Carter, you ever thought about participating in track and field?" the voice asked. As Tiu-Loo got closer, he could see that it was Coach David. "No sir, I've never really thought about it," Tiu-Loo replied. Tiu-Loo had no idea why he had asked him that question. Coach David was leaving school a little late when he saw Tiu-Loo jumping over the puddles. He couldn't believe that he could jump over what looked like six- and seven-feet wide puddles of water like that. Tiu-Loo made it look so easy to do. Kato didn't see what the fuss was about either. He was used to seeing Tiu-Loo run and jump daily. He never thought anything of it.

"Meet me in the morning. I have a proposition for you," Coach David said, as he let his window back up and drove off. Tiu-Loo and Kato looked at each other and continued walking home. Tiu-Loo liked sports, but he himself had never participated in any organized activities of the sort. His meeting with Coach David the following morning would prove to be a blessing in disguise.

"Come on, just try it one time. And if you don't like it, you can quit," Coach David pleaded, as he had been trying to persuade Tiu-Loo for the last 30 minutes. Tiu-Loo was okay with the idea of running, but he had no idea what long jumping was. Whatever the case, Coach David seemed deeply passionate about having him try it out. One plus that he had taken from the conversation was that the sport could possibly earn him a scholarship if he was good enough. After hearing Coach David spill his heart out, Tiu-Loo conceded. "Okay, only one meet. I'll do it." Tiu-Loo said, as he prepared for class. Even after agreeing to do the track meet, Coach David expressed to him the importance of coming to practice. Although the track meet wasn't scheduled until a few months later, he wanted Tiu-Loo to be prepared for what was to come. "Practice starts next week, right when school is over," Coach David said, as Tiu-Loo walked into the hallway.

As the next semester approached, the students prepared for prom and graduation. Tiu-Loo had improved his grade from a C minus to almost a B plus in his Calculus class. After several disagreements and many contemplations of quitting the track team, he eventually caught on to what Coach David had been trying to teach him. Tiu-Loo had natural leaping and jumping ability, but he lacked technique more than anything. After putting his pride aside and listening to Coach David, he had mastered his technique for his skill set. Tiu-Loo won first place in his track meet and did it with little effort. He was a natural, and by the end of his fifth meet, he had garnered ten scholarship offers from ten different universities.

Tiu-Loo had gained notoriety and was even voted in the top five most accomplished athletes in the state. He held the second-best record in the long jump at an impressive 25 feet and eight inches. That was incredible, especially since he had only been participating in the sport for a few months. The sky was the limit for him. He and Uncle Kobe would always end up doing an interview with the local news, or a sportswriter. Everyone was anxious to know what college Tiu-Loo would attend, but he wasn't going to make his decision until after prom.

It had been three months since the last time he had spoken to or heard from Nicole. His track schedule had kept him busy for most of the semester. Nicole had been working extra hours at her job while juggling school and her cheerleading schedule. The cheerleading squad had been practicing on a new routine to perform at the cheer competition that year. With their conflicting schedules, they were lucky to be able to cross paths during their normal school hours.

Tiu-Loo was sure that he wanted to ask Nicole to go to the prom with him. Whenever he would feel discouraged about approaching her, he would be reminded of what Kato had told him weeks before. "Say, boy-boy, if you don't ask her now, it's gonna be too late," Kato would reiterate. It had taken a while to build his newfound confidence. Most importantly, he wanted to show Nicole how his grades had improved due to her new methods she had taught him. He wanted to give her the proper credit that she deserved. For if it wasn't for her, there was no way he would've mastered Calculus the way that he did.

They had been texting back and forth on a Saturday afternoon. After an hour of exchanging words, Nicole decided to pick Tiu-Loo up from his home so that they could hang at her house. They had missed each other tremendously. They continued to catch up on things they had missed in each other's lives, as their schedules had kept them apart for a great amount of time. It was a twenty-minute drive that seemed to have lasted for three, because of the good time they were having while in route to Nicole's place. They entered the home and went into the living room.

There were trophies everywhere. She had been a cheerleader ever since the age of three. She had been dancing since she could crawl. They did the usual routine. She poured Tiu-Loo a glass of sweet tea, grabbed the mango oil from the countertop, sat on the couch, and proceeded to oil and massage Tiu-Loo's scalp. It was a feeling of absolute euphoria for him. She would massage and oil his hair with a soft and gentle motion. Her fingers were small, but strong. If there had been any tension in his body, it was eased by her hands roaming freely through his hair. Paradise was all he could feel whenever she would do that for him.

"This feels so good. I swear I could get used to this," Tiu-Loo said, as he closed his eyes enjoying the scalp massage. Nicole smiled at him and continued with what she was doing. Something seemed to be on her mind. They would talk about random subjects or critique the characters on one of their favorite television shows as they watched, but she was oddly silent during the process. A little concerned, Tiu-Loo turned around. "What's wrong? What's on your mind?" he asked, as he faced her. She looked away for a moment and exhaled, but no words came out.

He decided to ease the tension once and for all by manning up and asking her what he should have asked at the beginning of the school year. "I want to ask you a serious question," Tiu-Loo said. His heart started to beat rapidly. He didn't know what her reaction would be. The moment didn't seem any better as it was obvious that something had been heavy on Nicole's mind. He grabbed the glass of sweet tea and took a sip. As he placed it on the floor beside him, he could see that Nicole was waiting for the question he wanted to ask. "What's up?" she asked, as she put the top on the bottle of oil.

"Will you go to prom with me?" he asked. Nicole was overjoyed. "Of course, I'll go with you, Tiu-Loo!" she said, jumping into his arms, simultaneously wrapping her legs around him. She had waited all year for him to ask her. A couple of guys had asked previously, but she declined. She wanted to go to prom, but only if Tiu-Loo had asked her. Tiu-Loo was ecstatic to hear her answer. They smiled and hugged for a long time. Once they were done celebrating, Tiu-Loo told her about the ideas for their colors. They decided that black and red would be their choice. They were going to match perfectly.

"I thought you were gonna say no," Tiu-Loo said, as he pretended to wipe sweat from his forehead. Almost instantaneously, Nicole was reminded of why she had been distracted earlier. "I have something to tell you," she said, as she looked at him with distress. Tiu-Loo tried to grasp what he may have been in store for. He listened as she told him what her issue was. "I think our prom will be the last time we see each other. I'm going to bootcamp the week after, and I'm going to be away for a while," she said, as she watched Tiu-Loo's smile disappear. It was true. She had more than enough credit hours to get a certificate of completion from school, which enabled her to receive her high school diploma early. With her schedule being so conflicted, she didn't have enough time to inform Tiu-Loo about what she had been up to. She had no idea if she would have the funds for college, so when an army recruiter approached her about the opportunity, she went for it. At least she didn't have to worry about college anymore.

Tiu-Loo was devastated. "So just like that, you're gonna

up and leave? Wow!" he stated, as he pulled away from her. His eyes couldn't focus on her, as he was visibly hurt by the news he had just received. "I did everything I could do, love," she said, as she explained the many options that didn't seem to work in her favor before being forced to make her decision. She was determined to have a bright future. If that meant joining the military to achieve that goal, then so be it. Tiu-Loo hated the idea of her going to the Army, but he respected it. He knew the hard work she had put in and knew that she deserved a fair opportunity. "I'm so sorry, Tiu-Loo," she said, as she fell into his arms and cried. He held her tightly, as she sobbed uncontrollably on his chest.

They held on to each other, as if they were never going to see each other again. Tiu-Loo felt even worse, because he felt like he had failed at communicating with her during those months when they didn't talk. He would've been prepared and not hit with such a blow if he had known ahead of time. It didn't matter now. What was done had been done. He just wanted to make the best of the rest of the time they had to spend with each other. "Now, let's see what limousine service we're gonna use. You know we gotta make a grand entrance." Tiu-Loo said. Nicole looked up at him as she wiped her tears away and smiled. "That sounds like a great idea, love," she replied.

Chapter 4: Acting for Stage

His alarm had sounded off for the third time before he could wake up completely. "Damn it, I'm late again!" Tiu-Loo said, as he rushed to the bathroom to brush his teeth and put his clothes on. Adjusting to college life was a bit of a challenge for him. It wasn't like high school. He didn't have his Uncle Kobe there to wake him for breakfast or to let him know when he was running behind. College life had already shown him how fast paced things were. He was in a totally new and different world.

Tiu-Loo had managed to earn a full scholarship to Florida A&T. It wasn't as fancy as the major universities, but after taking a tour of the campus earlier that summer, he fell in love with what he had seen. The yellow and purple colors of the campus auditorium did the final trick for him. He knew that he didn't want to attend any other university.

He finished brushing his teeth and rushed to grab his books and shoes. To further complicate his situation, Tiu-Loo lived on the fourth floor of his dorm. It wouldn't have been as bad for him if the elevators had functioned properly. They were scheduled for maintenance before the semester began, but the process was yet to take place. This meant that Tiu-Loo would have to take the stairs and still run over to the opposite side of campus to attend his first class.

He decided to be a fulltime student and packed his schedule. His fifteen credit hours plus being an athlete would test his will power and patience. A few of the advisors warned him about taking on such a heavy load, but Tiu-Loo felt that he had things under control. As he ran across the campus, students looked on as he sprinted across the courtyard. He had hardly tied his shoes as one had nearly flown off his foot. When he arrived at his class, he quickly tied his shoes and walked in. As usual, the students were already on stage preparing their monologues.

Tiu-Loo was nearly 30 minutes late for his hour and a half class. "Mr. Carter, nice of you to finally join us," said Professor Hunt. The tall, baldheaded man had been a theater teacher for many years. He had a slightly low toned voice and was from the West Indies. A month had passed by, and Tiu-Loo was only able to be on time twice. His schedule was completely full during the day, plus he had track practice in the afternoon. By the time track practice was done, he'd finish late class assignments, shower, eat, then go to sleep. He had the same rigorous routine day in and day out.

"My bad, Professor Hunt. I overslept again," Tiu-Loo replied, as he put his books on the floor, and joined the other students on stage. Tiu-Loo initially wanted to major in accounting, but after seeing a stage play during his campus visit over the summer, he knew that theater was his passion. At the start of the fall semester, Professor Hunt called Tiu-Loo into his office. He urged him to wait until next year to participate in his acting class. He felt that Tiu-Loo wouldn't have the time to focus on the things that would help him make a passing grade. They went back and forth until Tiu-Loo convinced the professor to give him a shot. After a month of hardly any improvement, Tiu-Loo was already in danger of potentially failing the class. He was late almost all the time and could barely remember his lines whenever the class would rehearse for stage exercises.

Professor Hunt reminded him that he was in danger of failing his class. He could turn things around with the completion of his class projects and the play they were practicing on. However, showing up late would only lessen his chances of achieving that goal. Professor Hunt explained to Tiu-Loo that excuses were pointless. He motioned for him to get with his group and practice on rehearsing for the play that was scheduled for the end of the semester. While most of the students had monologues and character parts for the production, Tiu-Loo's job was a bit more complex.

He had a nice speaking voice, which prompted Professor Hunt to assign him to be the narrator of the play. He would also recite several poems that he would have to write himself. Although Tiu-Loo understood the pressure he could potentially be under, he accepted the role and challenge. He had a lot to prove, and he wasn't going to let his schedule prevent him from getting the job done. Tiu-Loo immediately joined his group and began practicing his lines.

He stumbled through a couple initially, but as time

progressed, he started flying through them with no issues. Professor Hunt was even surprised, as he listened in every few minutes to hear if Tiu-Loo had made any critical mistakes. He had been late, but at least he was improving with his stage presence and memory. The students in his group stood there admiring him, as he took his time to carefully memorize one of the poems he had written. They had never heard someone so young speak with such a wide range of words in that manner.

After completing his poem, the room grew silent. When Tiu-Loo was done, they all started snapping their fingers. That was the ultimate approval for a job well done by a poet. His words flowed naturally and were received by his classmates. "Now, if you could just be on time each day, that would be even more impressive," said Professor Hunt. Tiu-Loo let off a sigh and walked off stage. As he sat down, many of the students approached him to give him props on his performance. Not long after, Professor Hunt signaled for him to join him on the side of the auditorium.

"Mr. Carter, this stage production is going to be a very vital part of your grade," he said, while filing through his notebook that he was holding. "Yea, I know. I'm prepared for it," Tiu-Loo replied. The professor let him know that he was impressed by his poem but didn't feel that he would do a good job once the production was underway. "I guess I'll have to show you better than I can tell you," Tiu-Loo said, as he walked away. He grabbed his things and walked out once class had been dismissed. "Well, good luck," Professor Hunt said, as Tiu-Loo exited the room.

Tiu-Loo heard what he said as he walked out. He understood why the professor doubted him. After all, he didn't do a great job of holding up his end of the bargain. Being a student athlete meant more than just performing on the field. You had to go above and beyond in the classroom as well. Not to mention, those set of rules were also the requirements to keep and maintain his scholarship. He walked towards the student leadership hall, where he was greeted.

"What's up, boy-boy? You were late again, huh?" Kato had decided to attend Florida A&T along with Tiu-Loo as well. He had an opportunity to attend a college in North Carolina, but Florida A&T had a phenomenal psychology program that piqued his interest. Regardless of how popular he was, Kato maintained no less than a 4.0 GPA throughout high school. He had received his acceptance letter right around the time Tiu-Loo had received his. He wasted no time making his decision.

Tiu-Loo tried to laugh off Kato's question, but he was a little bothered. He could only drop his head as he and Kato walked through the building. "Come on, it can't be that bad, boy-boy," Kato said, as he tried to get Tiu-Loo to discuss what was on his mind. They made it to the student lounge and sat at one of the tables. It was a very welcoming environment where they would meet at least once a week.

Before Kato could ask, Tiu-Loo had already started to

express how he was feeling. "Man, this shit is harder than I thought it was gonna be," Tiu-Loo said. He went on to explain how he had set his schedule up, and how he thought he may be in over his head. After breaking down the pattern of his days, Kato reminded him of his suggestion weeks earlier. "I told you to do no more than twelve credit hours. You have too much going on, boy-boy," Kato said, as he pulled out one of the course curriculums. Tiu-Loo nodded his head and agreed with what Kato was saying.

"Yea, I don't know what I was thinking. Maybe I should drop some of the classes," Tiu-Loo replied. Kato advised him not too. Instead, he suggested that Tiu-Loo monitor his schedule and pay better attention to it. College wasn't going to be easy, but he didn't have to make it any more complicated than what it already was. Kato knew that Tiu-Loo would be okay once he started to manage his time properly. "'Preciate you, bro, for real," Tiu-Loo said, as he dapped Kato. Kato would always tell him the truth, whether he wanted to hear it or not. Tiu-Loo always respected him for that.

They sat and talked for a couple of hours until it was time for Kato to go to class. "I'll see you later, boy-boy," Kato said, as he grabbed his backpack and headed out. Tiu-Loo had gotten hungry since he missed breakfast earlier that morning. He decided to go to the cafeteria to grab something to eat. His stomach had been touching his back for the past hour and he could no longer take it.

Once he entered the cafeteria, he got in line and made his tray. There was always some type of activity happening in the student café. You had different cliques spread throughout the area; whether it was the fraternities, band members, or sorority members looking at themselves in imaginary mirrors, there was always energy in motion occurring. Tiu-Loo would often be curious as to what exactly the girls were looking at with the make-believe mirrors. It tickled him whenever he would see it.

As he sat down to eat his food, he was approached by a young man who had been passing out flyers. "Here you go. Hope to see you there," he said. Tiu-Loo gave a simple nod. He couldn't speak because of the food he had just stuffed into his mouth. After a few more bites, he flipped the flyer around and read the back of it. An event was taking place later that evening at the student courtyard for college freshman only. The guest speaker went by the name of Brother Malcolm. Tiu-Loo put the flyer aside and continued to dispose of his meal.

He hadn't participated in any extra-curricular activities on campus yet. His busy schedule wouldn't allow him to. He went and stood in line once more to get an extra plate. He had to be strategic, because students weren't allowed to bring food into the dorms from the cafeteria. He carefully put a few pieces of food onto his tray, walked over to his table, looked around to see if anyone had been watching, and emptied the contents into a plastic bag that he already had with him. After completing the task, he finished drinking the last of his juice, and was off to his English class.

The day had gone by rather quickly for Tiu-Loo. After his classes were completed, he had a brief meeting with his track coach, Coach Cameron. They discussed Tiu-Loo's future in track and with careful observation, Coach Cameron predicted that Tiu-Loo could possibly qualify for the Olympics if he continued to improve in the long jump. Tiu-Loo couldn't tell if his coach was serious or just boosting his head up, because it sounded too good to be true. He did a few jumps to warm up, before his coach had to leave practice early because of a family emergency. For the first time in the last month, Tiu-Loo was able to take a break. Having free time was starting to become nonexistent.

He went back to his dorm to take a shower and relax. After his shower, he went over a few notes from his English class and fell asleep within minutes. He didn't have a roommate, which enabled him to sleep with no distractions. Relaxation had finally found him after an earlier rough start.

The sun was still shining and pounding the pavement when Tiu-Loo fell asleep, but by the time he had awakened, nightfall was approaching. He went into his bag to retrieve the food he had taken from the cafeteria and placed it into the small refrigerator that was beside his bed. He received a notification from his phone. It was Kato telling him that he had gone on a date. That wasn't unusual for Kato. He had gained popularity on the campus as soon as he had arrived there.

Tiu-Loo was bored for the first time in a while and had nothing to do. He decided to straighten his room up a little. As he sorted his clothes out on his bed, he ran across the flyer that he'd been given earlier. The event was starting at 7:00 pm, and it was already 6:50. He figured it wouldn't hurt him to see what the hoopla was all about. He finished folding his clothes, got dressed, and prepared for the function.

As he approached the student courtyard, he found himself having to fight through the crowd to get closer. The courtyard was packed full of freshman students all eager to listen to the guest speaker. It was apparent that Brother Malcolm was a big deal. Tiu-Loo wasn't concerned about being on time, because he felt that it would be some type of fly by night event. He was wrong about his assumption.

All the seats had been filled that were set out earlier. It didn't seem to bother the other students, as the rest stood and listened to Brother Malcolm speak. He was a young, 26-year-old man who traveled to different college campuses to educate and motivate freshmen students. He annunciated every word, as he spoke directly to the students. Tiu-Loo was impressed with what he was hearing. He saw a lot of himself in the speaker.

He weaved through the crowd just enough to end up a few rows in front of the speaker. "You are in control of your own destination! Believe in your abilities and execute your plan!" Brother Malcolm said, as he continued to relay his uplifting message. The words would resonate with Tiu-Loo profoundly. Brother Malcolm was young, but seemed to possess the knowledge of an older, wise man. He was maybe 5'10 with a muscular build, like that of an NFL running back. When he spoke to the crowd, all eyes were on him.

When he concluded his speech, Brother Malcolm opened the floor for questions. He carefully listened to the students, as he patiently answered each one of them. Tiu-Loo had never seen anyone besides his uncle sound as smart and intelligent as Brother Malcolm. One thing he took away from his speech was when he heard Brother Malcolm say, "Control your life. Don't let life control you!" Tiu-Loo couldn't have agreed with him more.

Brother Malcolm took his time and greeted the students as he shook their hands. When he made it to Tiu-Loo, he congratulated him. "Hey, keep up the good work. You have big things ahead of you," he said. Tiu-Loo had no idea what he was referring to. "Thank you! Your speech was very motivating," Tiu-Loo replied, still unsure of what Brother Malcolm was talking about. As he moved on to the next student, Brother Malcolm smiled at Tiu-Loo and pointed his finger. At the end of the student courtyard stood a small billboard containing four pictures of the best athletes on the campus. Tiu-Loo's picture was one of them. He couldn't believe it.

He turned around and looked at Brother Malcolm, who in turn motioned a thumbs up at Tiu-Loo. At that moment, it dawned on him that he had no choice but to beat the odds. When he felt like his schedule had become overwhelming, Brother Malcolm's words had lifted him up. There was a mental and emotional recharge that occurred within him after hearing such a well delivered speech. Tiu-Loo was extremely glad that he had made the decision to attend the event. He learned things that he would never forget in life. One of the most important lessons was to never give up on yourself.

Newly inspired, Tiu-Loo prioritized his busy schedule, and took his time with it. He made it to class on time, practiced with the track team, and started going to bed at an earlier hour. He would set his alarm clock to wake him up 30 minutes earlier than his regular time each day; this would enable him to get dressed on time and make it to the cafeteria to eat breakfast in the morning. He stressed less and was able to focus on his theater production more.

Before he knew it, the end of the semester was upon him. The day had finally come to perform his part in the campus play that he'd been rehearsing for. Knots formed in his stomach as time grew closer and closer for the production. Not only did he have to memorize the poems he had written for the show, but he had to perform them in front of a large crowd. Tiu-Loo sat backstage and peeped out of the curtains, watching the seats in the auditorium fill up. Anxiety had fell upon him, but he continued to keep his composure.

He wasn't the only one who seemed to be nervous about the production. Professor Hunt, usually the calm and collected one, was slowly panicking as well. Every few minutes, he could be heard checking on things more than twice. "Make sure the lighting is good! How many people are out there now?" he would ask every five minutes it seemed. Tiu-Loo knew how important this event was, and failure on his end was not an option.

Most of the other students seemed to be ready to go. They had charismatic faces and ran around the backstage area as they wore their costumes. Many of them would go recite their lines to one another, before breaking off into small groups. Tiu-Loo believed that like himself, many of them were trying to ease whatever tension or nervousness they were feeling. It put his mind at ease, when he saw that they all were in the same boat. They were young adults who were ready to showcase their talents in front of their friends, families, and peers.

Tiu-Loo paced back and forth, as he recited the lines of one his poems to himself. Every time he would mess up, he'd start over until he got it right. He wouldn't allow himself to get upset. He was already nervous about having to perform in front of a live crowd. Professor Hunt had been observing Tiu-Loo for a while. He watched him recite his lines and advised him, saying, "Mr. Carter, if you make a mistake, just continue on as if nothing happened. Don't stall in the middle of your performance." Then the Professor continued to critique the other students who were practicing.

Tiu-Loo wasn't worried about his parts so much as he was about the crowd. He had never been put on the spot before. Participating in track and field events wasn't the same as performing in front of a theatrical audience. It was one thing to long jump on a field but acting on stage required another level of discipline and talent. Not only did you have to memorize lines, but you couldn't break character...not even a little bit.

He had done everything in his power to get himself prepared for this day. He rehearsed with other classmates and memorized most of the poems he had written. He was confident about the progress he had made and would soon find out if the hard work had paid off. The auditorium was packed with guests, and it was time for the stage production to begin. The students huddled up in one big circle, said a prayer for good luck, and it was off to the races.

As the play began, Tiu-Loo sat backstage patiently, waiting for his time to narrate and present himself to the audience. Each student went out and executed their role without making a single mistake. Before it was time to go out onto the stage, Professor Hunt approached Tiu-Loo once more. "Are you ready to perform?" he asked, as he stood in front of him. "As ready as I'll ever be, sir," Tiu-Loo replied. Professor Hunt nodded and walked off. He had seen the improvement that Tiu-Loo was making in his class, but he still wasn't convinced. He doubted if Tiu-Loo would've had time to memorize so many poems in such little time.

The last scene had ended, and it was now time for Tiu-Loo to go on. He rubbed his hands together and said to himself, "Here goes nothing." He entered the stage and was immediately stunned by how many people were sitting in the crowd. He scanned the crowd briefly and almost giggled as he was looking at the right side of the room. Kato had managed to make eye contact with Tiu-Loo and made a funny face at him when their eyes connected. Tiu-Loo took a deep breath, looked at the crowd, and recited his poem word for word.

When he was done, the audience clapped loudly, and they gave him a standing ovation. He had delivered each word brilliantly and hadn't missed a beat. He could hear Kato over everyone as he shouted over the crowd, "That's what I'm talkin' about, boy-boy!" He was moved by the poem that Tiu-Loo had just performed. Tiu-Loo was relieved that the hard part was over. This particular poem he performed was one of the newer ones he wrote a week before the production was supposed to take place.

As the play went on, Tiu-Loo's confidence began to grow more. He was precise with his words and the crowd loved every poem he performed. Once the play ended, the students lined up on stage and took a final bow. The audience was more than satisfied with what they had seen. The crew members hugged and conversed, as they talked about their favorite parts of the show. Many of them were amazed at Tiu-Loo's performance. Like Professor Hunt, they had doubt about whether Tiu-Loo would be able to commit to something that demanded so much of him. Indeed, he had proven everyone wrong.

As the last crew members helped clean the stage, Professor Hunt pulled Tiu-Loo to the side. "I underestimated you, Mr. Carter. I must admit, I'm impressed," he said, as he shook Tiu-Loo's hand. The weight had been lifted. Tiu-Loo wanted to prove his professor wrong, and he did. "Thank you. I worked very hard to get ready for this," Tiu-Loo replied. Professor Hunt congratulated him on a job well done and vanished backstage. The night was still young and some of the students decided to go to a restaurant. Kato walked down the aisle to see if Tiu-Loo was ready to leave. "Aye, boy-boy, dinner on me. Let's roll," he said. "Let's do it!" Tiu-Loo replied, as they followed the rest of the crew outside.

Chapter 5: Eye of The Beholder

The Annual Everglade Classic had just ended, and the celebration was about to begin. The Florida A&T Jaguars were victorious once again, as they pummeled the Jacksonville A&T Crocs, 88 to 53. The opposing team was no match for the Jaguars. Basketball season was underway, and Florida A&T had a formidable team. They were projected to win the conference title at the beginning of the season. Although the Crocs were last year's champions, they came up way short in their first game against the Jaguars.

As they left the arena, Tiu-Loo and Kato trailed the school shuttle bus back to campus. The game was a little more than an hour away from the city. As they arrived on campus, a car full of young ladies parked beside them. They waved and smiled as they exited their vehicle. Kato waved back, but Tiu-Loo just sat there as if he didn't see them. One of the young ladies tried to walk on the passenger where Tiu-Loo was sitting, but he immediately got out and started walking towards his dorm. "Hey, where you goin', boy-boy?" Kato asked, as he wondered why Tiu-Loo had taken off so suddenly.

Tiu-Loo kept walking, while Kato stayed behind to fraternize with the ladies. "What's wrong with your friend? Why'd he just take off like that?" One of the young ladies asked. "I don't know. Maybe he's scared of y'all," Kato replied, laughing and shrugging his shoulders. It was quite common for a young lady to approach Kato, but Tiu-Loo was a different story. He had been so focused on completing class assignments and track practice. Any activities outside of that would just have to wait until he had time for them. "That's okay. I'll see him around. Tell him I said hello," one of the young ladies said, as they got back into their vehicle and drove off.

Kato walked towards the dorm, assuming Tiu-Loo had gone upstairs to his room. As he got closer, he could see Tiu-Loo peeping his head around the corner. He found his behavior to be kind of strange. "Aye, boy-boy, are you crazy? Man, those girls were feelin' us!" he said, as he looked at Tiu-Loo for an explanation. "I was in a hurry, man, my bad," Tiu-Loo said, as he looked once more to see if the coast was clear. "In a hurry to do what, boy-boy? Come over here in the corner and hide?" asked Kato. Tiu-Loo tried to respond, but Kato wasn't trying to hear it.

They made it to Tiu-Loo's room, where Kato decided to interrogate him a little more. "So, what was the problem? Were they ugly or something?" Kato asked. Tiu-Loo could see that Kato wasn't going to let it go until he had given him an honest and valid answer. "I mean, come on bro. Four white girls parking beside us, and then all of a sudden, they wanna talk? Nah, I'm good bro," Tiu-Loo replied, as he grabbed two sodas from his refrigerator. "Yea, they wanted to talk alright. Talk about how much of a good time we were gonna have until you got ghost on me," Kato said, unscrewing the top on his soda to take a sip.

Tiu-Loo kept quiet. Kato asked him why he was in such a rush to leave the car, but Tiu-Loo wouldn't respond. Many young ladies on campus had shown interest in Tiu-Loo, but they would never approach him. They would flirt or speak every now and then, but it was nothing serious. "Do you not like white girls or somethin', boy-boy?" Kato asked. He was trying to understand what Tiu-Loo had been thinking. Tiu-Loo pulled out a newspaper article and read it to Kato.

The article talked about how white women would purposely go after athletes to somehow trap them later. There was a story about a Caucasian woman who purposely dated a star basketball player, got pregnant by him, and later, she put him on child support. She didn't really like him. She just wanted his money and the fame. Although he wasn't a basketball player, Tiu-Loo was well aware of his status as a track and field star. He promised his uncle that he would be careful with himself and girls while he was away for college. He didn't know the true intentions of anyone and didn't want to risk his career finding out.

"You're paranoid, boy-boy!" Kato said, as he laughed at Tiu-Loo. He agreed with his point but felt that most of the young ladies on campus just wanted to have a good time. They weren't thinking about having babies. They just wanted to party and hang out from time to time. Tiu-Loo listened but stood strong on how he felt. He had come too far to lose everything that he had worked for by being involved with the wrong girl or crowd.

After further discussion, Tiu-Loo had calmed down. "She had the hots for you, boy-boy. I'd say something to her If I were you," Kato said, as he described how pretty the young ladies were. "Man, I'm good. I'm gonna let you have it," Tiu-Loo said, as he assured Kato that he wanted no dealings with any of the young ladies. Kato shook his head as he grinned at Tiu-Loo. "Just don't do the weird peeking around the corner thing again," Kato requested. Tiu-Loo walked Kato into the hallway and told him to be safe while driving. Kato's mother helped him rent an apartment that was ten miles away from campus. He was used to being alone and didn't like the idea of having a roommate.

Tiu-Loo placed the newspaper article on his desk and pulled out his orientation book. He had an exam for his student orientation class that he'd been studying for. He tried to read a couple of paragraphs, but all he could think about was the young lady who tried to get his attention a few hours prior. Yes, he was being cautious, but he couldn't help but notice how beautiful she was. He thought about what college she may have attended. He had no recollections of ever seeing her on campus. As he pondered, he got on track and continued to study for his exam.

One afternoon after track practice, Tiu-Loo decided to go to the school courtyard to write a little. Whenever he had the time to spare, he would open his notebook and write a few poems. Some would be long, while others were short like a haiku. It was beginning to sprinkle rain drops outside, which forced him to retreat to the steps of the student café. The area was covered from the weather, making it accessible enough for Tiu-Loo to continue his writing. His first poem was about nature. As a child he loved to look at the animal channel, because of his infatuation with lions and tigers. He completed the poem with ease but began to have writer's block while writing the second one. He tried to find inspiration, but nothing would come to him.

The rain began pouring down heavily as lightning followed. He grabbed his notebook and entered the student café. It was filled with students patiently waiting for the rain to go away. They crowded the walkway and doorway, nearly forcing Tiu-Loo to push through them in order to find a seat. Once he matriculated up to the front of the café, he sat down and continued to write. He made it through a few lines on his paper, until he was tapped on the shoulder.

"Hey, what's cookin', good lookin'?" the young lady said, as Tiu-Loo turned around. When he looked back, he had to do a double take. She stood over him with her long, black hair and light-blue eyes. She had a feminine, but fit body frame, and stood about 5'5. Her smile complimented her pearly, white teeth. She had on a small hint of red lipstick, and a very mature demeanor. "Hey, what's up? Am I in your seat?" Tiu-Loo asked. The young lady responded, "No, but I'd like to know what you're so scared of." He knew exactly what she was referring to.

She was the same young lady who tried to introduce herself to him a few weeks prior, until he took off like a bat out of hell. "I'm not scared at all," Tiu-Loo replied, as he continued to be drawn in by her charismatic smile. "Well, I'm Holly. Do you mind if I sit down?" she asked. Tiu-Loo pulled out a chair to assist her, as she joined him at the table. It turned out that she attended the same university. She had a backpack and a purple umbrella in her hand. Once she sat in down beside him, Tiu-Loo started to introduce himself.

"My bad. My name is..." he began but was stopped in his tracks. "Chase 'Tiu-Loo' Carter," Holly finished. Surprised that she knew his name, he asked her how she knew his information. "I mean, come on. You're only one of the top track-and-field athletes in the entire division, and your theatrical poems are like visual scenes from a movie," she stated, leaving Tiu-Loo in disbelief. He wondered who this young lady was that had known so much about him. He immediately started to remember the article that he had shown Kato, and instantly became defensive. "So, what! You stalkin' me or something??" he said, as he closed his notebook.

"Of course not. Look at this," Holly said, pulling a piece of paper from her backpack. She handed it over to Tiu-Loo. It was a school newspaper article about his many accomplishments leading up to his arrival at Florida A&T. One of the school writers attended the theater production that Tiu-Loo had performed in. She was so moved by his poems, that she decided to write an article about him. Tiu-

Loo was never told about the article, because no one could really get in touch with him other than Kato. After the stage play, he went back to studying and going to track practice.

He stared at the article in amazement. Everything that was written about him was true and factual. "I'm sorry for yelling at you. I just don't trust many people," he said to Holly. She accepted his apology and didn't take it to heart. She was familiar with the student/athlete process, and how opportunistic some people could be. "If you would allow me, I'd like to tell you more about myself, if that's okay," Holly said, as Tiu-Loo continued to read the article. He stopped reading and obliged her request.

She took her time to explain her upbringing to him. She was from St. Louis, Missouri and was the youngest of three children. Her mother was a Navy veteran, while her father was a diesel mechanic. After her mother left the military, she graduated from nursing school. Like her mother, Holly's major was nursing as well. It was her junior year at the college, and she was excited about what her field of study had to offer. Tiu-Loo listened to her go on about how her parents preferred her to attend an Ivy League school, and how they wouldn't pay for her college if she had chosen anything other than what they wanted. Her story was interesting to say the least, but Tiu-Loo was still curious. As she continued with her story, he stopped her in the middle of her sentence.

"Excuse me, but what made you approach me?" he

asked. No one on campus had ever done that before. "Oh, Tiu-Loo, I've had a crush on you ever since I saw you on that stage." She, too, had attended the production and was blown away by the poem Tiu-Loo had recited. Holly was in the second row of the auditorium and could see everything up close. She even recited some of what she remembered from the poem. Tiu-Loo was at a loss for words. He didn't realize that so many people had been so entertained by his performance. He was just trying to ensure that he didn't have a failing grade for the semester.

"Women must throw themselves at you a lot, right?" Holly asked, with a look of certainty on her face. Tiu-Loo didn't respond. He went through the grueling process of describing his earlier childhood, and Holly was mortified. Hearing about what Tiu-Loo had gone through made tears form in her eyes. "Oh, it's all good. I accept myself for who I am," he said, as he tried to lighten the mood. He didn't want his story to be a Soap Opera episode. She learned a lot about Tiu-Loo, as he continued to open himself up more.

They conversed for a long time, but the elephant in the room had not yet been identified. Of course, Tiu-Loo felt it coming much sooner than later. After a few more trips down memory lane, it finally came to a head. "By the way, why did you disappear like a ghost that night I tried to approach you?" Holly asked. Tiu-Loo grinned because his prediction was correct. "Honestly, I was just nervous," he replied. He didn't think someone as beautiful as Holly would ever take an interest in him. The fact that she was white only heightened his anxiety even more. She continued to talk with Tiu-Loo about the last time she had seen him. "I was a nervous wreck. When I saw you at the classic, my heart just melted. You looked so damn good to me!" Holly said, as she reminisced about that night. At first, Tiu-Loo thought she was exaggerating, but as time went on, he could tell that Holly was really into him. It was more than some fan who was star struck.

Holly was enjoying her talk with Tiu-Loo. He seemed to be transparent with her. He didn't want her to leave without revealing one last thing, however. He let her finish her statement and made a startling confession. "I've always felt a way about my dark skin," Tiu-Loo said. He went in depth about how he was teased a lot because of it. That was another reason why he didn't want her to approach him that night in the parking lot. He went on to tell her about how ugly he thought he was, and how her having an interest in him was an unusual thing.

"Well, I think you're the most handsome man I've ever seen," Holly said. She pointed out the fact that his hair was long and beautiful. She would see him walking the campus sometimes, and marvel at how his hair would sway from side to side. She really wanted to know more about Tiu-Loo and offered to take him out on a date. She asked him if he would be okay with going out for dinner the following weekend.

"I don't know, I'll think about it." Tiu-Loo said, as he

grabbed his notebook. The rain had died down and the students were starting to exit the café. Holly wasn't sure if Tiu-Loo would take her up on the offer, so she made one more suggestion. "We can eat at any restaurant you choose. It'll be my treat," she said, as she smiled at him. He didn't want to turn her down, but he still had reservations about her intentions. She was being so nice and generous, that he didn't know what to think.

As they walked outside, she thanked Tiu-Loo for talking with her. Before heading to her next class, she gave Tiu-Loo her phone number. "You can call me anytime you want," she said. Holly hugged him tightly as if she didn't want to let go. Other than Nicole, Tiu-Loo had never shown public displays of affection with a young lady. The hug had thrown him off initially, but he managed to relax and hug her back. She told him to consider her offer once more as she departed.

Later that night, Tiu-Loo sent Kato an urgent text. He wanted to meet with him as soon as possible. Without any questions, Kato showed up to Tiu-Loo's dorm. When he arrived, Tiu-Loo was already standing outside. He didn't know what the sense of urgency was about, but he knew that it had to be something serious. "What's up, boy-boy? You good?" Kato asked while approaching Tui-Loo. "Not really," Tiu-Loo replied. Kato was starting to get worried. He thought that Tiu-Loo was having academic problems or worse.

However, that wasn't the case. Tiu-Loo wanted his

advice about going on a date with Holly. That would be his first time going out with a young woman who wasn't his friend. He informed Kato about the interaction that he had with Holly in the student café. Not only did they discuss their lives, but she offered to take him to dinner. After telling Kato about his encounter, Tiu-Loo asked if he should take Holly up on her offer. Kato assured him that if he did, he wouldn't regret it. Besides, not too many women would offer to pay on the first date.

"You know you could've just called me, right?" Kato said, as he continued to give Tiu-Loo advice about his date. He knew he could've reached out via phone, but he wanted Kato to be there and to see his true reaction. He didn't think that Kato would have believed that he was going on an actual date with someone. Kato told him to relax and go with the flow of things. He teased him about running away that night Holly tried to approach him and wouldn't let Tiu-Loo forget about it. The hard part was over. He had already been invited, which meant that he didn't have to go out of his way to ask her first. Attending a simple dinner and conversing wouldn't be so bad.

Kato suggested that Tiu-Loo call her right away to accept the invitation. Tiu-Loo mentioned that he would do so the next day, once he was able to be alone. However, Kato wasn't buying it. "Nah, boy-boy, call her right now, while I'm standing here," Kato said, as he smirked and folded his arms. Tiu-Loo had run out of excuses, and Kato wasn't going to let him slide that easily. Tiu-Loo had his phone in his hand. He scrolled through the contacts until he found Holly's. As he highlighted her name, he looked over at Kato once more. The look on Kato's face wasn't changing. Tiu-Loo understood that it was now or never. He made the phone call.

After the second ring, Holly answered. "Yea, about dinner…I'd be happy to go with you," Tiu-Loo said in a low voice. Kato leaned in closer to hear what Holly was saying, but her voice was too soft. She told Tiu-Loo that she would pick him up on Saturday and to have an appetite. "Sounds great!" Tiu-Loo said, as he ended his call with her. He exhaled a sigh of relief. Kato gave him high-fives and joked with him about how nervous he was. Tiu-Loo was about to go on a date and with a very attractive lady at that.

After their mini celebration, it dawned on Tiu-Loo that he didn't have anything to wear. He wore clothes to class, but nothing fit for a date. The wardrobe in his closet wasn't quite up to par. "Damn, what am I gonna wear?" he asked Kato. Kato already had him covered. He pulled out his phone to show Tiu-Loo a few pictures of his clothes. "Man, this is the one," Tiu-Loo said, as he pointed out a blue blazer from the lineup of pictures that Kato had shown him. "Cool, I'll bring it by after work tomorrow, boy-boy," Kato replied. That problem was solved. Now, all Tiu-Loo had to do was follow through and not stand Holly up on their first date.

Saturday had come in no time. It was a beautiful afternoon, and Tiu-Loo was ready. He ironed his clothes the night before and matched the blue blazer with blue slacks and a crisp, white shirt. His long locs hung down his back with a rubber band securing the base and middle of his hair. He had a nice pair of dress shoes that his uncle bought him on the day of his graduation. He had received a text an hour prior that Holly would be on her way shortly to pick him up for their date.

He headed downstairs to meet Holly in the parking lot of his dorm. As he walked by, a few of the students had to look twice. They had never seen Tiu-Loo dress up before. "Okay, lookin' dapper as ever," one of the young ladies said, as he strutted towards the crosswalk. He had a different swagger about himself. He was just in time. Just as he was about to stand near the steps of the parking lot, Holly was pulling in.

When she parked the car to get out, Tiu-Loo was mesmerized. She sported a nicely fitted blue dress, with black heels that matched her black hair. He was taken aback even more because of her shape. He couldn't tell she had curves when they were in the student café, but indeed, Holly was stacked. "Well don't you look spiffy," she said, as she walked over to hug Tiu-Loo. They complimented each other well. She asked Tiu-Loo if he would like to drive instead. She had been at the gym earlier and her legs were sore from her intense workout. Tiu-Loo didn't mind. They walked back to Holly's car. Tiu-Loo opened the door for her, and they were on their way.

"I hope you're hungry, because I'm starving," Holly said, as she turned the radio on. Tiu-Loo nodded his head and rubbed his stomach, indicating that he felt the same way. They talked until they made it to their destination. The restaurant wasn't what Tiu-Loo expected it to be. When they arrived, valet was offered immediately. Holly handed over the keys to one of the drivers, as they stepped out of the car. The facility was obviously upscale. There were chandeliers hanging from the ceilings, and the waiters and hostesses all had on tuxedos. "You sure we're in the right place?" Tiu-Loo asked, as the two were being led to their table.

The waiter passed them the menu and Tiu-Loo was even more surprised. The prices were a bit higher than the ones he had seen at other restaurants. There was a steak that was priced at 75 bucks alone. "You can order whatever you'd like," Holly said, as she continued to look through the menu. "Are you sure?" Tiu-Loo asked. The prices on the menu didn't seem to get any lower. Holly told him to eat as much as he wanted. She wasn't concerned about the price. Although her parents didn't want her to attend Florida A&T, they still gave her a monthly allowance. Her scholarship, along with the money that she was receiving from her parents, allowed her to be a little more comfortable than others.

A few minutes went by before they both agreed that the filet mignon was going to be their meal of choice. The waiter brought sweet, Hawaiian bread rolls and fresh lemonade to their table as appetizers. There was a lit candle on their table with a complimentary rose beside it. It seemed to be the tradition of the restaurant because there was one placed at each table. The atmosphere was peaceful, with dim lights all around.

Holly had the medium-rare filet mignon, while Tiu-Loo had his well done. Very little was said, as they went on to eat their meal. There was an assortment of different steak sauces at the table ranging from mild to spicey. Tiu-Loo had no idea that Holly could eat the way she did. It made him even more comfortable to see her in her element. Kato had mentioned on several occasions that when he would take a young woman out, she would act shy and not want to eat her food in front of him. Holly was doing the total opposite. She wasn't playing about her appetite at all. She had finished her plate and was already ordering dessert. Tiu-Loo on the other hand, was just now making it to his steamed vegetables.

"What would you like for dessert?" Holly asked, wiping the steak sauce from her lips. Tiu-Loo told her that he would have what she was having. She ordered two hot brownies with vanilla ice cream to top it off. After dessert, Tiu-Loo expressed his gratitude. No one had ever done that for him before. While Holly did pay for dinner, Tiu-Loo insisted that she let him pay for dessert and take care of the tip. The waiter was very courteous and polite. Holly tried to convince Tiu-Loo not to pay, but he had already beat her to it.

He let her know that the meal was splendid and that he wouldn't have to eat for the rest of the day. They were all smiles as they sat at the table, drinking the last of their lemonade. "We should do this again sometime," Holly said, as they prepared to leave. Tiu-Loo agreed with her, but only under the condition that she allowed him to pay for the next meal. She had been looking at his hair the whole time. She asked him how long it had been since he started growing it. "Since I was three maybe," Tiu-Loo replied. "Well hopefully I can play in it sometime," Holly said, as they made it outside to wait for valet to pull her car around.

He smiled at her and let her know that it could possibly happen one day. With her legs still being sore, Holly asked if Tiu-Loo would drive back to campus. He started to become a little concerned, but she assured him that she would be good enough to drive home. Her apartment was off campus. However, she didn't live too far away. As Tiu-Loo drove back to his dorm, Holly thanked him as well. She wanted him to know that she appreciated the thought and effort he put into their date. She was also relieved, because she didn't think he would want to go out with her.

The sun was setting by the end of their trip back to his dorm, and Holly asked if he would like to hang out at the park soon. Tiu-Loo didn't see a problem with that. After all, he had gone on what he thought was an expensive date, but still had an amazing time with her. "You really wanna continue seeing me?" Tiu-Loo asked. "Of course, why wouldn't I?" Holly replied. Aside from a few outings with her friends, she had no social life. School consumed much of her time and there was no young man in her life at all. In fact, she was such a bookworm that her parents had to beg her to attend her own prom.

They sat and talked in the parking lot for a while. As they said their goodbyes, Holly asked Tiu-Loo if he was okay with dating her. She was very forward and direct about her intentions. She had feelings for him, but she didn't want to force anything. "I don't know. I guess I'd have to think about it," Tiu-Loo said, as he soaked in what Holly was asking. They embraced each other and gave their salutations for the evening. Before getting into her car, Holly made a bold move. As Tiu-Loo was staring at her, she leaned in and kissed him on the lips.

She looked up at him and waited for his reaction. "Whoa! Definitely wasn't expecting that," he said, as he stepped back. A kiss was the last thing that he had anticipated at the end of their date. Not that he didn't want her to kiss him, he just didn't think that Holly was that attracted to him. She held her head down as if she were ashamed to have made such a move without warning him. "Hey, it's cool. You just caught me of guard a little. That's all," he said, as he put his hand under her chin, tilting her head upward. Holly apologized for kissing him, but Tiu-Loo let her know that everything was fine.

He was no kisser. In fact, he had never kissed a girl in his life. The occasional Nicole cheek kiss would happen, but it was nowhere near the lips at any time. He wanted to tell Holly to kiss him once more, but he was too embarrassed to ask. He figured he'd save her the trouble of going through the mechanics of kissing. He surely didn't want the reputation of not knowing what to do when it came to being intimate with a young lady.

"You're just so handsome. I couldn't resist the temptation anymore," Holly continued. Tiu-Loo smiled and thanked her for the compliment. He let her know that he would be texting her later, and that he was looking forward to hanging out at the park soon. He would have more time to enjoy himself, because his freshman year was coming to an end, which meant that he would be free most days during the summer. They were going to bond more for sure.

Chapter 6: Psycho Drama

"**S**mack my ass harder!" she demanded, as the other guy sat across the room to wait his turn. The two basketball players had been in the hotel room for roughly 45 minutes, having their way with Laziah. A nineteen-year-old freshman who grew up privileged and spoiled, she seemed to always get what she wanted. Boys would flock to her. She was light-skinned, with a nice shape. She had pretty, brown eyes and shoulder length hair. Her five- foot, three-inch body frame was nearly perfectly proportioned. Everything Laziah did was to her benefit, or to seek attention. She wanted to stand out as much as she could. If that meant dimming another person's light to shine, then you'd better run for cover.

Laziah was raised in Miami, Florida. She had a Dominican father, and African- American mother. Her parents were both lawyers, but her father was also the acting pastor at the church they attended on some Sundays. It wasn't abnormal for the family to attend church almost every Sunday out of the month. Consequently, this caused Laziah to be rebellious at times. She became very promiscuous at an early age. By the time she was thirteen, she could already fit into a size 32DD bra. Her parents sheltered her for most of her life, and the only time she could go out was with relatives or close friends who her parents had already known about.

At the age of fifteen, Laziah was invited to a Purity Ball by one of the young ladies who attended her church. The ceremony was intended to be for young ladies who wanted to pledge their celibacy until they were married. The intention and idea were great, but Laziah was a year too late. A few weeks after her 14th birthday, Laziah snuck out of her house to attend a party. Once she got there, her high school crush, Milo, began to flirt with her. He, too, had just celebrated his 16th birthday around the same time as Laziah. After whispering something into her ear, Milo led the more than willing Laziah upstairs into one of the bedrooms. She lost her virginity shortly after. She was sneaky enough to where her parents never found out about her transgressions. She kept her grades up in school, she used protection, and she hardly ever missed curfew.

As she looked at her cell phone, Laziah told the two basketball players that they only had a few more minutes left with her. She had to meet with a couple of her group members to discuss a skit that they had been practicing on. She was big on acting. From elementary on into high school, Laziah had participated in every musical and theatrical production that she could. She loved the attention and more importantly, she loved the break that it gave her from her parents. It was no surprise that theatre was going to be her major upon entering college.

As she grabbed her things to go into the restroom, one

of the players let out, "Damn, I still had one more nut left," as he touched himself while looking at Laziah's half-naked body. "I'm about to take a shower. You can watch me if you want," she replied, as she went into the bathroom to turn the water on. The two ball players looked at each other, and they rushed into the bathroom to have a front row seat of her display. She had a tattoo of two cherries on her upper, right thigh. She lathered her body up slowly, putting on a show for ball players.

Laziah finished her shower and got dressed. She wore a blouse, reading glasses, casual boots, and a small jacket. The boys stood and looked at how dramatic her transformation was. They would've never guessed that she was as freaky as she was by how she looked. Initially, she would give off the shy, preppy girl vibe. However, once she was comfortable, she would reveal her true identity, but only if she wanted to. She may have been a little loose with herself, but discretion was still the name of her game.

She got into her car and headed to campus. As she drove, she applied a touch of lip gloss to her full lips. She preferred a more natural look, so only a little eye shadow from time to time would suffice. When she arrived, she spotted one of her group members. Notrice, a light-skinned girl from Arkansas had just came from her dorm to meet with the group as well. She had beautiful green eyes, long, red hair, was very soft spoken, and had the patience of a grandmother. Many of the group members were already tired of Laziah trying to run things, but Notrice would simply ignore it and try to find a solution to the issues at hand.

As she parked her car, Notrice motioned for Laziah to meet her at one of the tables near the student café. The sun was shining bright, and the 77-degree temperature had it feeling just right to be outside. They sat down at the table to discuss the latest ideas for their upcoming skit. The semester was fresh, but Professor Hunt was already administering assignments for his newest students. Laziah wanted to do a skit that focused on men worshiping women, while Notrice wanted to focus on more of a comical aspect of things. Either way, the group would still have to vote and go with the skit that had been chosen unanimously.

They sat at the table and brainstormed, as they waited for the other group members to arrive. Not long after they had started the process, Laziah took notice of the young man with long dreadlocks walking down the steps from the student café. He was accompanied by a young lady who had been holding his hand the whole time. "Damn girl, who is that!?" asked Laziah, gazing at him walking across the courtyard. "His name is Tiu-Loo. I think he's on the track team or something," Notrice replied.

"He can be on my track team any day. I love me some chocolate! Lawd!" said Laziah, as she continued to stare at him. While she did go after any and every young man that she wanted, she had an affinity for darker guys. As a child, one of her favorite celebrities was a dark, muscular actor who starred in a catalogue of movies. Since then, her ideal boyfriend was one who possessed those qualities, at least the skin tone part. Laziah continued to go on about what she'd do to him if she had the chance to get him alone. After Notrice mentioned that he had a girlfriend, Laziah dismissed her statement. "Who? The white girl? She doesn't even know what to do with him," she said, as the other members of the group were starting to arrive.

Before the other two members made it to the table, Notrice had convinced Laziah to do the comedy skit. It was no hard feat, because she agreed to let Laziah choose the skit for their next project. They all conversed until Juwan, a football player and theater major, mentioned the new production that was taking place at the end of the semester. "Tek Weh Yuhself" was a new musical that Professor Hunt had been working on with another student. Juwan explained to the group that auditions would be held soon, and anyone was free to tryout. Laziah took notes and put the information into her calendar. If there was an opportunity to be in a play or showcase, she wasn't going to miss it.

They wrapped up their meeting and Laziah walked to the student café. She wasn't hungry but wanted to acquire some information. One of the ladies who served food in the café was taking her lunch break. As she pulled out a chair to sit down, Laziah approached her. "Excuse me, would you happen to know how often the guy with the long dreads comes in here?" she asked. The woman was puzzled. She had seen many young men with dreadlocks enter and exit the café that day. "I wouldn't know, baby. There are plenty of them around here," the lady responded, as she opened her bottle of water. Laziah caught an attitude with her, because she didn't hear the answer that she was looking for. She didn't thank the lady or anything. She just turned around and stomped off, exiting the café. "She's like a spoiled kid in a candy store," one of the students said, as they watched the conversation take place.

She was determined to get close to him and wouldn't stop until she did. As Laziah walked to her dorm, one of the fraternity brothers handed her a flyer. There was going to be a big celebration off campus, and he wanted her to come by. Perry was a senior in college and had been a member of the fraternity since his sophomore year. A tall, light-skinned man with gold teeth, and tattoos on his body, he was one of the most eligible guys on the campus. "You make sure you bring that body tonight, shawty," he said, as Laziah smiled and agreed that she would attend the party.

She went to her room and sorted through her closet. Most of her wardrobe came with matching outfits, shoes included. She decided to wear a fitted pink dress for the occasion. She ordered Chinese food and relaxed on her bed until it was ready to be delivered. Many of the freshman students weren't allowed to attend the frat parties. This enabled Laziah to be herself and attract the attention that she desired. Whatever she would choose to do off campus would be left there.

After eating her Chinese food and having small talk with her roommate, it was time to get ready for the party. Laziah carefully put on her eyeliner and added a small touch of makeup. She grabbed one of her heavy coats from her closet. She didn't want anyone to see her yet in the revealing dress that she chose. Once she made it to her car, she put the address into her GPS and got on the road.

Upon making it to the event, Laziah was a little thrown off. She had made it safely, but all she could see was a bunch of land, with lights that seemed to lead to nowhere. Not knowing what to expect, she began to drive off. Before she could get a chance to leave completely, a man appeared in the distance. He slowly walked towards her car. He had on black jeans, and a white tank top. As he got closer, she could see that he had a cane in his hand with the fraternity logo on it. "Hey, go this way love," the man said, pointing Laziah in the right direction.

As she drove into the darkness, she could see that it wasn't a regular house party. Instead, the fraternity had rented out a barn for this particular event. When she got out of her car, she noticed a hand full of people were at this party, with only five girls, including her. As she walked towards the barn, Perry approached her. "What's good, shawty? I see you made it," he said, as he escorted her inside. There was a single file line of five young men standing inside the barn. They had on green shorts and white tank tops. They were blindfolded with a chair placed in front of them.

Perry went over to the ladies and made an announcement. "Say, some freaky shit about to go down, so if you ain't wit' it, you free to leave. Ya dig?" He gave the ladies time to think about the things that were about to happen. None of the ladies left, so Perry proceeded with the first activity. Perry had the ladies choose a guy of their choice. Laziah couldn't see his face, but she liked the tall guy with the nice haircut, and waves in his head. She stood next to him and waited for further instruction. Perry told them to help the guys sit in the chair that was in front of them.

Once they sat them down, Perry passed out five pieces of chewable, fruity candy. He told the ladies to be as nasty as they wanted to be, or they could simply be PG about the situation. Laziah immediately started rubbing and kissing on her partner's neck. He instantly became erect because of her soft lips and intimate moans. As she continued to tease him, she whispered in his ear, "I'm the queen of this freaky shit." The young man replied, "Well show me somethin' then." The other ladies were entertaining their partners as well. Some even stripped down to their panties to give lap dances.

As Laziah felt the bulge in her partner's shorts, she put her hands inside them, and started massaging him. Seeing that Laziah was about to take it to the next level, Perry quickly grabbed a huge blanket to cover her head. Completely tuning everyone out around her, Laziah began performing an orally charged sex act on her partner.

Luckily, none of the other girls could see her, as they were too distracted to pay any attention. It only lasted for a few minutes, as her partner's leg started to shake. "Hey, you okay?" she asked, as she peeked from under the blanket. "Hell yea! It just feels good, that's all," he replied.

She helped him fix his pants, as Perry prepared to stop the time. He asked everyone if they were having a good time and was answered by handclaps from everyone. Once the guys were standing up again, Perry told them to remove their blindfolds. The guys hugged the young ladies and thanked them. Perry walked over to Laziah and asked her partner how he was feeling, being that he had gotten some special treatment. "Man, I feel good, boy-boy! I can't wait to cross over," he responded. The young men were getting prepared to be the newest members of the fraternity soon. They were just one more initiation and ceremony away.

"I'm glad you were satisfied," Laziah said, as she hugged her partner. "Oh yea, more than satisfied. I'm Kato, by the way," he replied. Perry helped everyone to their cars and made sure they made it into the street safely. As Laziah got ready to leave, Perry complimented her performance. "You got skills, shawty. Thanks for comin' through," he said, as the barn lights made his gold teeth glisten. She smiled and headed back to campus. She went to bed that night feeling like she was on top of the world. She had just hung out with some of the top and hottest fraternity guys on campus. She felt that she could literally have any guy she set her sight on.

The following week, Laziah was with her group. They performed their comedy skit in front of their professor and peers. They were greeted with a standing ovation at the end of their performance. Once they were done, Professor Hunt told everyone to take a seat on stage. He had an important announcement to make, but he was waiting for another student to arrive. Everyone waited anxiously, as they were eager to hear the big news that Professor Hunt had to tell them.

It wasn't long before the student he was waiting on walked into the auditorium. Professor Hunt met him on stage as he addressed the rest of his students. "Everyone, this is Chase Carter. He'll be helping with the casting of the new production that we're doing this year," Professor Hunt announced, introducing him to the students. Not only would he be a part of the casting process, but he would also co-star in the production as well. Once Professor Hunt was done speaking, Chase took the floor to elaborate more on the subject.

"You guys can call me Tiu-Loo," he said. He held a stack of papers in his hand. He informed the students about the auditions that were going to take place. The papers consisted of the names of each character, and the role they would play. Tiu-Loo also encouraged them to audition for multiple roles, and whomever was best would get the part. As Tiu-Loo stood there explaining the details of the production, Laziah kept trying to get his attention. She would make little noises and try to wink at him, but he just wasn't paying attention. As he concluded, he asked the students if they had any questions for him. Laziah raised her hands and asked what character he would portray in the production. "Well, that remains to be seen," he replied, as he looked on to see if any of the other students had more questions.

He passed out the papers, and let the students pick and choose the characters they wanted to portray. As the students went over the papers, Tiu-Loo chatted with Professor Hunt for a few minutes. He went over to the students and told them that the auditions would be held at the end of the week. Once the students made their selections, Tiu-Loo collected the papers and handed them to the professor. He proceeded to make his exit, as he walked up the aisle towards the auditorium doors. Seeing it as an opportunity, Laziah excused herself and followed behind him, as he made it into the hallway.

She quickly approached him. "Hey, I'm Laziah, I just wanted to say that you are sexy as hell to me," she said, as she bit her bottom lip. She told him that she would like to know him more and that she would love to braid his hair someday. Tiu-Loo thanked her and politely declined her offer. "Thanks, but I have a girlfriend. She's the only one who does my hair," he replied. Laziah felt slighted. Because Tiu-Loo didn't accept her invitation, she caught an attitude with him as well. "Oh, so that lil white girl got you whipped, huh? It's cool," she said, as she rolled her eyes in unison, while simultaneously pointing her hands in different directions. "Hell, it's whatever you wanna call it, but like I said, I'm good, love. Enjoy!" Tiu-Loo said, as he turned his back and walked away from her.

Laziah picked her face up from the floor and walked back into the auditorium. She walked down the aisle and sat with the rest of the students. Realizing that she had left suddenly, Notrice asked her if everything was okay. "Yea, I'm good, girl. I just had to go to the restroom. That's all," she replied. The students were excited about the upcoming auditions and began discussing the characters they had chosen to portray. "I'm definitely going out for the part of the French maid," Notrice said. Laziah stared at her with an unpleasant look. Of all the characters on the paper, she had only chosen one of them. "I'm auditioning for that part too," she said to Notrice. They both shook hands and wished each other luck. Laziah wasn't too concerned, because she felt that no one was better than her, acting wise. She had received praise from a few of the professors on campus for her acting ability and was sure that the part was already hers.

Later that day, Tiu-Loo was cuddling on the couch with Holly. She would come pick him up from campus after track practice and make lunch for him every now and then. They had gotten pretty serious since their first date and Tiu-Loo was with her almost every day. As they cuddled and watched the movie on television, Holly asked him about the progression of the new production he had been working on. He gave positive feedback. He talked about how excited the students were and how it would be a great opportunity for many of the theatre majors. Holly was thrilled to hear the good news. She admired how devoted Tiu-Loo was about his craft. Over the summer, he came up with the concept of the play. Once he was confident about his ideas, he ran them by Professor Hunt.

Impressed by the storyline and the brilliant ideas Tiu-Loo had presented to him, Professor Hunt accepted the play, and gave Tiu-Loo credit for his masterpiece. Not only were they going to present the new play, but Professor Hunt had invited several famous thespians as well. Tiu-Loo's performance the year before was well received. Many of Professor Hunt's peers were impressed with how well his students had delivered their performances. "Tek Weh Yuself" was going to exceed all expectations.

Holly supported Tiu-Loo every step of the way. She looked over his writing plans, helped make copies of programs, and even proofread the script for him. After reading over the script a few times, she knew that the play was going to be successful if executed properly. As Tiu-Loo was going over the details of the process, he had one small concern. He told Holly about the brief encounter he had with Laziah earlier. He mentioned to Holly that it was odd to him, because she knew that he was dating someone who was white. He had never seen or met her, so that threw him for a loop.

Holly laughed it off and told him not to worry about

it. She mentioned how the campus was like a small town and that the young lady may have just seen them around a few times. "Yea, the chick was just a weirdo to me," he said, as he laid his head into Holly's lap. She kissed him on his forehead and rubbed his shoulders and arms. In no time, Tiu-Loo was sound asleep. There was no place better than being in the comfort of his woman's presence.

The day for the auditions had finally come, and Laziah was ready to show out. Days prior, she could be found standing in the mirror of her room, reciting the lines she had memorized. She would walk the campus each day getting into character and making sure everyone could hear her French accent. She would go to her theatre class dressed in a maid uniform, while pretending to do chores after class had been dismissed. Auditions hadn't started yet, but she was prepared to get the role. Professor Hunt found it rather comical, but he appreciated her dedication. The other students liked her outfit but felt that her preparation for the role was a bit over the top.

As she prepared for her audition, Laziah said a few lines from the monologue that she had memorized. When she walked into the auditorium, she was taken by surprise. There were far more students there for the audition than she had anticipated. She didn't realize how much the other students had taken interest in the production. She knew that she had to put her game face on and knock her performance out of the ballpark.

The students were all lined up in separate areas of the auditorium, waiting on their names to be called. As she went to where the line was for the character of the French maid, Laziah could see that there were only three girls, including herself, that were auditioning for the part. She only recognized Notrice. The other young lady was fairly new. She was a theatre major but didn't attend Professor Hunt's class that semester. Giving a very dull salutation to the two girls, Laziah stood in line and watched the other actors try out for their respective parts.

The theater roared with thunder, as the students expressed themselves through their dialogue on stage. The auditions were bringing out the absolute best in some of the students. By the time the male auditions were done, many of the spots had already been filled. It was time for the ladies to get to work. Notrice was visibly nervous. Her hands were shaking, and she beat herself up repeatedly whenever she would forget one of her lines. She didn't have time to watch the other students, because she was too busy fumbling her words while practicing. Laziah had looked over at her a few times and laughed at the mistakes she was making. At one point, she even told her to wait until the next production to try out, because she clearly wasn't ready for this one.

Notrice paid her no mind, as she continued to rehearse by herself in the distance. Tiu-Loo and Professor Hunt sat at the end of the stage and asked the young ladies if they were ready. The first girl had excused herself, because she received an urgent phone call. She stepped into the hallway, but never returned for her audition. By rule, she had forfeited her chance to be in the production. Laziah was ready to perform her scene. Before Tiu-Loo could see who wanted to go first, she was already on the stage, front and center. Most of the students stayed behind to witness what was about to take place.

"Okay, let's begin, shall we?" said Professor Hunt. Laziah waited a few seconds to add a dramatic effect to her performance. She spoke loudly and fast, but everyone could keep up with what she was saying. During her audition, the students were still tickled at the fact that she was wearing yet another maid's costume. She traveled around the entire stage reciting and memorizing her lines. When she was done, she took a bow and exited promptly. "Pretty good," Professor Hunt said, as he signaled for Notrice to walk on stage. "That was pretty cool," said Tiu-Loo, giving her a thumbs up. She winked her eye at him and sat down with the rest of the students.

Notrice was nearly terrified after seeing Laziah's performance. Her feet felt like they were stuck in cement, as she walked across the stage. Tiu-Loo could see that she was uncomfortable. "Hey, it's okay. Just take your time and relax," he said, as Professor Hunt gave her the que to start. She took two deep breaths and mumbled softly. "Come on, you got this," she said to herself, as she began her lines.

She immediately grabbed the attention of everyone

in the auditorium. Normally a noticeably quiet and soft-spoken girl, Notrice could be heard in the hallways as well. Her voice carried over the entire room and before she knew it, she had concluded her audition. Everyone was at a loss for words. She had spoken so clearly, and her voice was strong and powerful. Everyone stood up and clapped loudly except for Laziah. She was so stunned while watching the performance, that reality had slipped away from her.

There was nothing to discuss. Notrice had earned the roll as the French maid for the production by a landslide. The students huddled around her praising her for what she had accomplished with her audition. "I didn't think I was going to do well," she said, as she celebrated. Tiu-Loo and Professor Hunt asked for everyone's attention. They had made their final selections on the spot. They thanked everyone for their participation and informed them that an official roster would be posted on the side of the stage on the first Monday of the next month.

Laziah was furious. She didn't believe that Notrice deserved to get the starring role. She had practiced for hours each day and felt that she was more than qualified for the part. She couldn't wait until the students left the auditorium. As Tiu-Loo and Professor Hunt were coming down from the stage, Laziah confronted them. "What did I do wrong? Why didn't I get the part!?" she asked, with an unsettling tone. Professor Hunt responded by letting her know that Notrice was simply better for the part.

She didn't like his answer. She became very loud to the point that Tiu-Loo had to interject. "Why are you being disrespectful? If you would've focused more on your lines instead of trying to dress like the character, then maybe you would've gotten the part," he said, defending his professor. It was true. Although she had done well on stage, she had also messed up on some of her lines. Whereas Notrice went through her performance flawlessly.

"This is bullshit!" Laziah shouted, storming towards the exit doors. The students ignored her as they exited the auditorium. Professor Hunt looked on and tried to forget about what had just happened. He gathered his things and headed backstage to his office. As she got closer to the doors, Laziah made one final declaration. "And you didn't even try to stick up for me. That's okay. You think you're all that, but I got you though!" she said, as she yelled at Tiu-Loo.

"You ain't got shit, stupid ass female!" Tiu-Loo replied, returning the same energy that had been given to him. He was fed up with how much of a downer she had been. He refrained from getting in the middle of things initially, because he didn't want to choose sides. However, her attitude was uncalled for. His uncle taught him to respect women at all times, but if they were to attack him for no reason, then he had a right to defend himself. Whether it be mental, physical, or emotional, Tiu-Loo wasn't going to tolerate one-sided aggression from anyone.

The students calmed Tiu-Loo down. They told him to just ignore her immaturity. "It's all good. I'm not worried about her," he said, as he grabbed his backpack. "Yea, alright," said Laziah as she walked outside. Tiu-Loo shook his head and answered his phone. Holly was waiting for him outside.

Chapter 7: Olympic Trials

"**G**ood job. Let's try to stick the landing next time, okay?" Coach Cameron said, as Tiu-Loo had completed his tenth and final jump for practice. He was having a record setting year in track and field and was slated to try out for the Olympics in the coming weeks. Coach Cameron was impressed with how much he had improved within the last year, but he still wanted Tiu-Loo to focus on his technique a little more. Tiu-Loo would practice hard, but he really didn't take the sport seriously. He was naturally gifted at his craft, which enabled him to win many of his competitions.

As Coach Cameron ended practice, one of Tiu-Loo's teammates approached him. "Yo, you better get it together. You only got one shot to make the team," he said, as he took off his spiked, running shoes. Tiu-Loo shrugged his shoulders and headed towards the locker room. He was very nonchalant about the sport. He always did his best, but whether he made the Olympics or not, didn't matter to him. He was just happy to have earned a scholarship and not have to pay for school out of his own pockets.

As Tiu-Loo disappeared into the locker room, his teammate continued to mumble under his breath. "Ole cocky ass dude! Wish he'd take his ass on somewhere!" he said. Emilio was embarking on his senior year in college and was determined to make his dreams come true. Born to Dominican parents, he lived and breathed track and field. His body was made for the sport. He was about 6'2, he had a long-lean built body, and massive top-end speed. He was light skinned with hazel eyes, and had a curly, high-top faded haircut. He also had a tattoo on his right shoulder that read "Victorious."

Unlike Tiu-Loo, track and field was Emilio's world. He won state championships in the long jump and triple jump competitions while he was in high school. In each of his three years at the university, he would fail to qualify for the Olympics, as he would fall short each time. Last year, he lost his chance to compete by a mere two and a half inches. During the summer, he had dedicated much of his time to work on his speed and long jumping abilities. He would go to the track and practice for hours. At times, Coach Cameron would catch him napping on the bleachers. He was hell bent on qualifying and didn't want to fail this go around.

Although he was faster than Tiu-Loo on the track, he was no match for him when it came to the long jump. Even as a freshman, Tiu-Loo would easily out jump Emilio by five to six inches during practice. Before Tiu-Loo joined the team, no one had given Emilio any real competition. He would become frustrated with Tiu-Loo at times because he knew that the sport wasn't much of a priority for him. He couldn't understand how someone was so good at something that they didn't even have a true desire for.

He'd often refer to Tiu-Loo as a cocky showoff whenever he would complete one of his jumps after practice. He kept his thoughts to himself. While he disliked Tiu-Loo, he would never tell him that to his face. He wanted to keep the peace out of respect for Coach Cameron, who by the way, was very instrumental in recruiting Emilio to attend the college. It was obvious that Tiu-Loo was a remarkable athlete, but he needed guidance. This prompted Coach Cameron to ask Emilio to mentor him occasionally.

He reluctantly accepted Coach Cameron's request, but only because he felt like he owed him. During his freshman year, Emilio had gotten into some trouble, because of a house party that he was invited to. He was drinking alcohol and ended up missing a very important track meet due to his hangover. After facing expulsion from the team, Coach Cameron decided to give him a second chance. In many ways, he felt that he was indebted to his coach, and didn't want to risk his career in the future.

He would show Tiu-Loo different techniques and become enraged in silence, as he would watch him master them. Not only did Tiu-Loo become more efficient during practice, but he would acquire more distance with his jumps. In due time, Tiu-Loo was going to be a force to be reckoned with. Emilio began to accept the fact that some athletes were simply born with certain abilities that even practice couldn't match. It didn't matter how many hours he would put in; he could never surpass Tiu-Loo.

Tiu-Loo went into the locker room to grab the rest of his gear before heading to his dorm. When he walked in, a few of his teammates were standing in a circle, along with Coach Cameron. He didn't pay any attention to what was going on. He continued putting his clothes into his duffle bag, as he cleared his locker. Many of the guys had funny looks on their faces. It was like they had found out about something but couldn't say anything until the time was right. Tiu-Loo had peeped the silence and slowly started to wonder what was happening.

"Where's Emilio?" Coach Cameron asked, as he pulled a stack of envelopes from a small bag he had been carrying. Tiu-Loo let him know that Emilio was still on the track, but that he was heading their way shortly. They waited a few more minutes, until Emilio joined them in the locker room. "Bout time you made it E," said one of the other teammates. Before Coach Cameron explained to the guys what was going on, he made a brief announcement. "I just want you to know that I am extremely proud of each and every last one of you!" Then he passed the envelopes out to them.

Tiu-Loo didn't know what was going on. Just like the rest of his teammates, he thought that Coach Cameron was about to pull some sort of prank on them. As he handed them out, he told each of them to wait until everyone had an envelope in their hand. "You fellas have worked so hard, and I'm honored to present this to you," Coach Cameron continued. By this time, the team had become very anxious. Whatever it was that was about to take place, had to be something major. The last time Coach Cameron had made a similar speech was the year before, when the team made it all the way to the city nationals.

"Okay, you can open them now," Coach Cameron said, as he could see the anxiety rushing forming on their faces. All at once, they opened their envelopes. Within seconds, there were a host of screams, chants, and high-fives being exchanged. They had qualified for the Olympic trials, which meant that they were one step closer to actually making it to the Olympics. Tiu-Loo was stunned. He couldn't believe what he was reading on the paper.

Although it was Emilio's third time being invited, he was still grateful. He had worked very hard over the summer and figured that the third time was the charm. "Man, this is amazing! Thanks Coach!" Emilio said, as he ran over to Coach Cameron and embraced him. There were two twin brothers, Alphonso and Alonzo, who were given invitations as well. They were dual sport athletes who had been recruited by Coach Cameron when they were only freshmen in high school. They had come from Nashville, Tennessee and were very dominant in their field. They specialized in the 100 and 200-meter dash. They usually would come in first and second place amongst each other. They were a little more emotional than the other guys, because their mother had passed away earlier that year.

Tiu-Loo was aware of his abilities, but never in life did he ever think that he would've accomplished such a seemingly impossible feat. Even as he read the letter and its contents, he still was in disbelief. "So, what does this mean exactly, coach?" Tiu-Loo asked. Before Coach Cameron could respond, Emilio had already beat him to it. "It means that you're about to have the opportunity of a lifetime, so don't blow it," he said, as he continued to celebrate with his other teammates. Coach Cameron nodded his head and gave a fist bump to Emilio.

Who would've thought that the dark-skinned "jungle boy" from Alabama could potentially be an Olympic hopeful? Tiu-Loo concluded reading his letter and thanked his coach before departing. He could only think of one person the entire time he had received the news. He walked into his dorm and proceeded to make a phone call. The call went to voicemail initially, so he waited until he made it to his room to try again. When he tried it a second time, the person on the other end picked up.

"Hey, what's up man? How are you?" Uncle Kobe asked. Tiu-Loo was happy to hear his voice. He would text every now and then, but due to both of their conflicting schedules, they hardly ever got a chance to talk on the phone with each other. "Man, Uncle Kobe, you won't believe what just happened! I was just invited to try out for the Olympics!" he said, as he could hardly contain himself. Uncle Kobe was excited for him. He told him that he was proud, and that he would try his best to make it if he could.

They talked and caught up, until it was time for Uncle

Kobe to get back to work. "Your mother would've been so proud of you. You have her strength and determination for sure," Uncle Kobe said. Tiu-Loo told his uncle that he loved him, and he ended his phone call. Uncle Kobe's words were always uplifting. Tiu-Loo looked at his bracelet on his wrist and thought about his mother. He wondered what it would be like if she had been around to see the many things that he was accomplishing. With the schedule that he had, he didn't believe that he would be able to keep up in college. Yet here he was, about to take on the world and its competitors soon.

Across campus, Emilio was having his own celebration. He had broken the news to his fellow fraternity brothers, and they all decided to have a small gathering in the student café. Perry had ordered pizza and chicken wings for the occasion. He made a couple of phone calls, and before you knew it, all the fraternity brothers from the campus had shown up to congregate in the student café with him. They had on their green and white boots, and made a huge spectacle of themselves, as they performed a few steps for the ladies who were in the building.

As they continued with their gathering, Kato, one of the newest members of the fraternity, had finally arrived. He didn't know what the purpose of the meeting was. All he knew was that he had received a text while he was at home, advising him to show up to the student café at once. He walked in to see his frat brothers, and asked Perry what was the reason for the meeting. They were all eating pizza by the time he had made it to one of the tables.

"Yo' Perry, what's really good?" he asked, as he greeted him with their secret fraternity handshake. Perry informed him that Emilio was on his way to participate in the Olympic trials soon. Kato immediately went over to congratulate Emilio. "Congrats bro. I wish you the best while you compete. That's Major!" he said, as he shook hands with him. They all sat down at the table and ate their food. One of the ladies that were there started to ask questions about the process of making it to the trials. Emilio elaborated as much as he could. He was happy about being chosen to compete, but it was his final remark that would spark a misunderstanding.

"I'm feeling good about the trials, but this black ass dude named Tiu-Loo needs to stay out of my way," he said, as he continued to eat his pizza and wings. After hearing that, Kato quickly responded. "And what's the problem with Tiu-Loo exactly?" he asked, taking his shades off to look Emilio in his eyes. Everyone at the table stopped talking, realizing that Kato was serious. "I mean, the man barely gives any effort at practice. Coach acts like he's a savior or some shit! He really should be thanking me for even getting as far as he did," Emilio said, as he took a sip of his soda. The people at the table nodded their heads, indicating that they agreed with what Emilio was saying.

Kato didn't like what he had heard at all. Although they were on different paths, he and Tiu-Loo were still best friends. They didn't see each other every day, but they still hung out whenever they could. Kato wasn't about to let anyone speak badly about him, frat brother or not. He looked around the table and spoke clearly. "Tiu-Loo is a hard worker, he doesn't owe you anything, homie," Kato said. Not liking what came out of Kato's mouth, Emilio stood up from his seat and yelled across the table at him. "Bro, what the fuck did you just say!?" "I said he don't owe you shit, hoe ass boy! And we can throw hands about this shit! Fuck you talkin' bout!?" Kato threatened, as he started to remove his shirt.

Everyone moved away from the table expeditiously. Kato had balled his fists and began hitting his knuckles together. As he started walking over to Emilio's side, Perry intervened and broke it up. "Say man, what are y'all doing? Y'all brothers, shawty." he said, as he made sure distance was kept between them. Kato calmed down and explained to Perry that he simply didn't tolerate disrespect. He understood that they were a part of the same fraternity, but Tiu-Loo was his real brother.

"It's not even that serious, man," Emilio said, as Kato walked away. Kato didn't want to hear what he had to say. He felt that the fraternity was supposed to be about unity and helping all brothers. He wasn't a fan of contributing to the tearing down of another man, least of all one that he had an actual bond with. "You gotta watch what you say sometimes. You don't know who knows who around here," Perry said, as he advised Emilio to start thinking before he decided to speak on something or someone.

"Man, fuck him. I'm 'bout to enjoy myself," Emilio said, as he sat back down to finish the rest of his soda that was on the table. One of the young ladies who witnessed the altercation, walked up to Emilio's table, and offered to refill his cup. "Would you like more, daddy?" she asked, as she flirted with him. "See, I ain't trippin', dog," Emilio said, while looking up at Perry. The young lady refilled his cup and promptly sat down in his lap.

Still furious about what had just transpired, Kato decided to give Tiu-Loo a call. When he answered, he let him know about the argument he had with Emilio. "Wassup, boy-boy! So, this dude was about to see all five of my knuckles in his face!" he said, while explaining the incident. Tiu-Loo listened carefully to what Kato was saying. It was all new to him. The Emilio that he had known was not the one that was being described to him on the phone. He couldn't believe the things he was hearing, but he knew that Kato wouldn't lie to him about it.

"Did he tell you that I was selected for the Olympic trials?" Tiu-Loo asked. Kato stopped what he was saying and told Tiu-Loo to repeat himself. After he reiterated the news to him, Kato congratulated him. "That's what I'm talkin' 'bout, boy-boy! You know we gotta celebrate right!?" he said, as he continued to praise Tiu-Loo for the accomplishment. Tiu-Loo thanked him and told him that he wanted to hang out soon. He had already told Holly the good news, and she wanted to do something special for him. "Yea, just watch out for dude, boy-boy. There's somethin' up with him," Kato warned. Tiu-Loo assured him that he would investigate the situation as soon as he could. He had no idea there was an issue between him and Emilio.

As night fell, Tiu-Loo became restless. He tried to go to bed early, but it backfired. His talk with Kato earlier had been heavy on his mind. He didn't understand why Emilio had said those things about him. He went over everything in his head, and just couldn't pinpoint where the issue could've stemmed from. He listened whenever Emilio made suggestions, and more than anything, he was always respectful. He looked up to Emilio, because of the many things he had learned from watching him on the field. Trying to figure out what the problem was only gave Tiu-Loo a headache.

He looked at the letter from earlier and read it once more. He realized that he could possibly be a part of history. No one from his university had ever made it past the trials. They had all fallen short for their respective reasons. He got out of his bed and started to get dressed. It was the middle of the night, but he didn't care. He was headed to the track to practice on his long jumping techniques. If he was going to make it to the Olympics, then a little more practice would be necessary.

As he walked on campus, he held a piece of paper in his hands. Coach Cameron had written down the distance he had cleared at his last track meet; 27 ft and 4 inches was the distance. Coach Cameron felt that he could easily improve by at least a foot more. Once he made it to the track, he put his spikes on and walked onto the field. After stretching and a couple of warm up sprints, he was ready to work on his technique.

Every jump he attempted started off strong, but he felt that he was lacking proper execution. He would think about Coach Cameron's advice: "Run fast and finish strong," Tiu-Loo had decent speed but would sometimes pull up a little early before jumping. He took the piece of paper to mark the spot on the field that represented his best jumping effort. Making it to his starting point, Tiu-Loo took off with his first attempt. He dropped his head from disappointment with the jump. He didn't have anything to measure his distance with, but he was sure that his jump was well under 26 feet.

He continued to repeat one jump after another. He was slowly gaining momentum and feeling better about each attempt. As he was 'bout to attempt another jump, someone shouted across the field. "Hey, you can't be out here at this time," the person said. It was nearly pitch black in Tiu-Loo's area. All he had was a dim stadium light that gave off just enough power so that he could see the field. Tiu-Loo squinted his eyes, but still couldn't see anyone. As he tried to make out the voice of the individual, a short, heavy set man slowly appeared.

It was Mr. Salter, the head of campus security. When he realized that it was Tiu-Loo, he changed his tone. "Oh Tiu-Loo, it's you. I thought one of these kids were up to no good," he said, as he shined his flashlight. The week before, one of the sororities decided to do a hazing event that had taken place on the track. Mr. Salter rounded up the ones he could catch. For taking part in an activity that had been banned by the university, the young women were expelled.

"What's up, Mr. Salter? I'm just getting a little practice in," Tiu-Loo said, as he tried to control his breathing. He was nearly exhausted from his attempts and didn't realize that an hour had passed. Sweat dripped down from his face as he continued to gather himself. "It's all good. I know the big day is coming soon. Go ahead and finish up. I'll wait for you," he responded, putting his flashlight away. He wouldn't have to wait long; Tiu-Loo was tired. He'd given his all trying to reach his mark. He grabbed his belongings and walked off the field with Mr. Salter.

"Hey, don't overwork yourself. You're gonna be fine. Trust your abilities," Mr. Salter said, as he encouraged Tiu-Loo. He offered him a ride back to his dorm on the go-cart he was riding, but Tiu-Loo opted to walk instead. "Thanks, Mr. Salter, but I'll walk. I need to clear my head anyway," Tiu-Loo replied. Mr. Salter drove off and continued to do his rounds on the campus. As he walked, he thought about the track meets he had in the past. Although it wasn't his passion, he knew that he wanted to be great at the sport. He also understood that he could be the very best at it, if he put in the work. After practicing on the field and doing it the way Coach Cameron had been trying to teach him, Tiu-Loo understood the process. From now on, he was going to destroy the competition.

The day for the trials was approaching, and the practices were becoming very intense. Usually, Emilio would be one of the teammates who would give advice or motivate others. However, he was very reserved and secluded. He would perform his duties and go off into another direction by himself. He didn't want to be bothered by any of his teammates. Whenever someone would try to ask him a question, he would act like he didn't hear them. It was easy for him to do because he kept his headphones on while practicing. If you tried to get his attention, he'd simply turn his music up and continue with what he was doing. It didn't bother Tiu-Loo at all. He was already aware of how Emilio felt about him. Kato's words didn't fall on deaf ears, and Emilio's actions had given him all the proof that he needed.

During one practice in particular, Emilio was being very passive aggressive towards Tiu-Loo. Every other statement was a smart remark, or an improper suggestion that had been made. He decided to show off the fact that he had perfected his technique in the long jump. It was impressive. He had been practicing intensely and it showed. He improved by jumping nearly a foot and three inches past his season's best. When Tiu-Loo would practice his jumps, Emilio would critique his every move. "You definitely won't make the Olympics with that distance," he would say, whenever Tiu-Loo would complete one of his rotations. He didn't like Tiu-Loo, and Tiu-Loo was aware of it. He was focused on the task at hand, and nothing would keep him from what he was trying to achieve.

The track team had been preparing for weeks, and the big day was only 24 hours way. Coach Cameron had all the guys take a knee, as he went over the rules with them. "Remember, once you get there, you're not allowed to leave for any reason," he stated, as he covered each of the rules twice. He didn't want there to be any reason for a potential disqualification. He wanted everyone to show up 30 minutes ahead of time to ensure that they were checked in and accounted for. After dismissing the team, Coach Cameron asked Tiu-Loo and Emilio to walk around the track with him. He wanted to make sure they were ready to compete.

As they walked, he let them know that they were the ones he counted on the most. They had strong leadership abilities and their teammates looked up to them. He continued to praise them for setting the bar and maintaining their strong, competitive spirits. Coach Cameron could tell that Emilio didn't want to be there. He seemed agitated and uncomfortable. "Is there anything wrong, Emilio?" Coach Cameron asked. He could see the frustration on his face. "I'm just ready to compete, and walking around this track talking to you won't help me be anymore ready than I already am. No offense coach," he said, as he stopped walking. Coach Cameron nodded his head, and excused Emilio. It was unlike him to be as uneasy as he was, but Coach Cameron just assumed that the jitters of the trials were getting the best of him.

"Don't worry, coach. I won't let you down," said Tiu-Loo. Coach Cameron expressed to him that holding back would not be an option. "I want you to give it everything you've got. Don't hold back! Not even a little bit, you hear me!?" he said, as he stressed the importance of Tiu-Loo's full potential being tapped into. He encouraged him to get a good night's rest and to avoid any distractions for the rest of the day. Tiu-Loo shook his coach's hand and completed the last lap around the track with him as they walked.

As he crossed the field, Emilio gave them a rather dirty look while their back was turned. "Ima show his ass what's up! He won't even be in the top five when I'm done with him," Emilio said. He was done with masking his true feelings. He was going to make the Olympics and do away with any doubts once and for all. His jealousy and envy had consumed him completely. Not only did he want to prove that he was the best athlete on the field, but he also wanted to show Tiu-Loo that he was no match for him.

It was 9:00 am and the first event wasn't starting until 10:30 am. Tiu-Loo had his gold and purple warm-up track suit on and had been sitting on the bleachers with Kato. He was nervous, but calm. He watched as the other athletes entered the gates to register themselves for the competition. There were people from all over the country. There was a concession stand where the vendors sold food, and Kato was already craving an order of nachos. "Aye, boy-

boy, I'm about to go grab some nachos. You need anything?" he asked. Tiu-Loo declined his offer. He didn't need to eat anything before his competition.

Kato walked down the bleachers and headed over to the concession stand. Before he could get in line, a crowd of at least fifteen individuals had entered the gates. They were chanting and holding signs with green writing on them. Leading the pack was Emilio. He had invited some of his fraternity brothers and their closest associates. When he saw Kato, he tried to speak, but Kato ignored him. He had no words for him since the argument that had taken place in the student café. Even if the fraternity had meetings, he would make every effort to not interact with Emilio. His vibe was never right, and Kato wasn't cool with that.

Once he got his nachos, he hurried over to sit with Tiu-Loo. "Man, I'm gonna beat his ass before it's all said and done!" Kato said, as he dipped one of his chips into the hot cheese. Tiu-Loo laughed at him but knew that he was serious. As time went by, the events had taken place. It was time for Tiu-Loo to get ready for the long jump competition. Emilio had been on the other end of the field getting prepared. His frat brothers were praising him and gave encouraging words of thought. "You got this, shawty. Go get what's yours," Perry said. It was time to prove that he had what it took to make his dreams come true.

As Tiu-Loo started walking down the bleachers, a man called out to him. "Hey man, knock 'em dead out there!" "Uncle Kobe, you made it!" Tiu-Loo said, nearly tripping over one of the bleachers trying to greet his uncle. He wasn't sure if he would make it, because of his busy schedule. Every time he would ask him if he could come, there was never a definitive answer. He hugged him tightly and thanked him. He was so excited that he didn't realize Holly was standing right behind him. The weeks leading up to the trials were very busy for Tiu-Loo. He had given Holly his uncle's number in case of an emergency. While Tiu-Loo had been preoccupied with practice, Holly and Uncle Kobe were already planning his trip to Florida. When Uncle Kobe arrived at the airport that morning, Holly was already there to pick him up.

"Good luck baby. I'm so proud of you," Holly said, as she kissed Tiu-Loo. He headed down to the track and mentally prepared himself. He had done all the training that he could do. Coach Cameron was sitting in the front row. He gave Tiu-Loo a thumbs up and continued to survey the field. Tiu-Loo took deep breaths and exhaled slowly. He adjusted the bracelet on his wrist, said a prayer, and put his game face on. The announcer made the final call for the long jump competition, and the competitors lined up to get ready.

One by one, each competitor executed their jumps. When Tiu-Loo made his first attempt, he stunned the crowd. He had jumped an impressive 27 feet and five inches. That put him in second place, right behind Emilio who had jumped two inches further. The crowd went crazy as Tiu-Loo was shocked himself. Coach Cameron shook his fist and smiled while cheering Tiu-Loo on. As the competition progressed to the last round, it came down to the final three competitors. There were only two spots left for the Olympic team, so the process of elimination had begun.

Emilio started off strong, but he hadn't done better than his first jump in the earlier round. He was hanging on by a thread. Jay, a Junior from Jacksonville A&T, had jumped the same distance as him in the second round. It all came down to one final jump. Jay was first. He ran down the field and jumped an astounding 27 feet and nine inches. That jump automatically put him in the lead. It didn't phase Emilio. He knew that he could jump further if he took his time. Tiu-loo had jumped 27 feet and 6.5 inches, but that was just enough to keep him in the conversation. Emilio knew that he couldn't go past that.

He took off running with his eyes glued to the ground. When he landed, the judge ruled that he had jumped a personal best of 27 feet and eight inches. He had jumped just an inch under Jay. Emilio's fraternity brothers went crazy as they yelled and screamed. Tiu-Loo dropped his head. He felt that he had given it all he had and there was nothing left. He had competed at the highest level.

Coach Cameron waved at Tiu-Loo to get his attention. "Run as fast as you can. Don't let up until the last second. You can do this. Get out of your own head!" he said. Tiu-Loo got himself together. It was his last jump, which meant that the competition wasn't over just yet. Holly, Uncle Kobe, and

Kato all sat in the stands with their hearts racing rapidly. Tiu-Loo started at the mark. He put his head down and stared at the ground below him. He took off with blazing speed and left his feet in a swift motion.

The crowd went bananas! He had set a new championship record that stood for over six decades, with an official distance of 29 feet! It was such a rarity for someone who had never competed in any major competitions to achieve such an incredible milestone. He had out jumped everyone on the field, and most importantly, he had secured his spot on the National Olympic Team. The other athletes rushed over and congratulated him all at once.

Kato, Uncle Kobe, and Holly screamed to the top of their lungs, as they read his name on the big screen in the stadium. Chase Carter was going to the Olympics and no one could take that away from him. As the competition ended, the stadium started to clear out. Tiu-Loo had already left with his loved ones, but the fraternity members were still on the bleachers. Emilio was heartbroken. He was so close to making it, but still came up short. As he confided in his friends, a young lady consoled him. "Hey, that's okay, big cousin. You did the best you could do," she said. "Nah cousin, that's bullshit. I'm tired of him being in my fuckin way constantly! I need to do something about him ASAP!" Emilio said. Laziah had been there the whole time in support of her big cousin, Emilio. She was willing to support him on whatever he wanted to do. "Just tell me what the move is, and I got you," she said, as she did their

141

family handshake with him.

Chapter 8: The Set Up

It was a little past 7:00 pm, when a man driving a red Mercedes pulled into the parking lot. Lil Painty, a known drug dealer in Florida, had been asked to meet at a local gym. As he parked his car, a young man wearing a hoodie opened his passenger door and got in. "So how many of these do you think I should get?" he asked. Lil Painty looked at him and laughed. "Say rem, this must be yo first time doin this?" Lil Painty asked. He could see the uncertainty on the young man's face. After pulling his hoodie off, Lil Painty recognized who he was.

"Emilio!? Man, what the hell you doin' buying these!?" he asked; he was referring to pills. They were called "Mitchell Roddy" pills. Considered very lethal in some instances, the pills made you dizzy before ultimately knocking you out for hours on end. He didn't have time to go into detail. "Just tell me how much so I can go. Alright!?" Emilio said, as he kept looking around to make sure no one was in the area. Lil Painty gave him four pills for 80 dollars and sent him on his way.

Emilio put the pills into a paper towel that he had and walked back into the gym. He was finishing an intense workout that he had started an hour prior. He went into a bout with depression following his defeat at the

Olympic trials. He didn't want to hang out with his friends, and he had started abusing alcohol. Before he spiraled completely out of control, Coach Cameron referred him to the campus psychiatrist. After a few therapeutic sessions, she encouraged him to workout in order to relieve some of the anger he was filled with. It helped him a little, but he was still disappointed in himself for failing to qualify. After finding out that Tiu-Loo had purposely been holding back at practice, he was even more furious with him. Knowing that Tiu-Loo was better than him, even at his worst, was just a reality that Emilio didn't want to face.

The semester was coming to an end, and it was time for him to figure out the next phase of his life. Most of his time was put into track and field, but he did manage to keep his grades up. He would be graduating soon, with a degree in education. Most nights would be long, as he would stay up for hours on end. Defeat left a very sour taste in Emilio's mouth. Eventually, someone was going to have to pay for it, and that someone would be Tiu-Loo.

When Tiu-Loo returned to campus from the trials, he received a hero's welcome, including receiving an invitation to eat dinner with the Dean of the university. Being a part of history had catapulted Tiu-Loo into instant stardom. When he would go to the local restaurants, people would offer to pay for his food. They would even ask to take him shopping. The fame was quick and sudden, but he handled it in a very mature way. Tiu-Loo would have to turn down the offers because it was against the rules for college athletes to receive money or charity. However, Uncle Kobe could accept money, and put it into a trust fund that Tiu-Loo would have access to later in his life.

The front office of the dorm was filled with fan mail from people all over the world. For days on end, the dorm director and his assistant would have to spend an extra hour just to prepare Tiu-Loo's mail. Many of the students either wanted an autograph, or at least a picture with him. He never let the fame get to his head. He was very humble and appreciative for all the great things that were occurring in his life. He knew that he had accomplished something that very few people in the world could ever say they did.

It was the month of May, and the students had been preparing to get ready for the summer. Holly was excited because she was graduating soon. The Olympics had been set for August, which gave her time to spend with Tiu-Loo. He had been busy with interviews throughout the week. She didn't want to interrupt his process, but Holly had been waiting patiently to have some alone time with him. It seemed that after class each day, there was some reporter with a microphone in his face. They all seemed to ask the same questions such as, "Do you think you'll win a gold medal at the Olympics?" Holly knew that he would end up being busy at times, but she didn't want him to become overwhelmed.

When she was finally able to catch up with him, they were able to have their time alone with each other. An occasional lunch date or walk in the park would always be refreshing. Holly wasn't sure where she would pursue her residency for nursing, but she wanted Tiu-Loo to be there with her every step of the way. She didn't care where she ended up; as long as he was by her side, she was just fine. Of course, Tiu-Loo was down for whatever. She had shown nothing but patience and loyalty to him, and he was forever grateful for the love and bond that they shared. There was no way that they were going to be apart.

During the final week of the semester, there were a ton of events and parties taking place. Different organizations walked around the campus passing out flyers and giving personal invites to their official celebrations. There were pajama parties, sorority, and fraternity get togethers to name a few. Tiu-Loo had been invited to several of them, but his plan was to spend his last few days with Holly. They had mapped out a few activities that they wanted to do with each other before it was time for them to part ways.

One day, Tiu-Loo was walking to the auditorium to meet with Professor Hunt. He wanted to discuss a possible production that he wanted to put on for his Junior year. Being a sophomore in college wasn't as hard as his freshman year was. He had caught on quickly and was ready to embark on a serious journey into the acting and theatre world. As he continued to walk the yard, he was approached by Emilio. It was unusual and odd, because they hadn't exchanged any words since their meet at the trials. "What's up? How you been?" Emilio asked. "I'm blessed. What do you want?" Tiu-

Loo asked. He really didn't have anything to say to Emilio.

Seeing that Tiu-Loo wasn't being receptive to him trying to converse, Emilio handed him a flyer. "What is this for?" Tiu-Loo asked. He looked at the designs on the flyer. The letters were in green and white, the color of the fraternity that Emilio was a part of. "I just wanna end this beef between us. You're more than welcomed to come if you want," Emilio said. The flyer had the names of the athletes who had made it to the Olympics. Tiu-Loo was the only one in the long jump category, but Alphonso and Alonzo had also qualified in the 100-meter dash. As he read the flyer, he had mixed emotions about it. "Now why would someone who obviously doesn't like me, want me at their party?" Tiu-Loo asked, as he folded the flyer and put it into his pocket.

Emilio explained to him that it was all just a misunderstanding. He told him that he was just under a lot of pressure and didn't want to fail. He even went as far as showing him one of his slips from his many sessions that he had taken with his therapist. He was putting a lot of effort into showing Tiu-Loo that his intentions were pure. "Just think about it man, and congratulations on making the team, too," Emilio said, as he walked off. Tiu-Loo didn't know what to think. He had seen Emilio several times on campus since they had returned, and he never made any attempts to have words with him. Something didn't seem right, but he didn't have much time to ponder on it.

When he made it to the auditorium, he couldn't do

anything but laugh. There was still a huge banner hanging over the front of the stage that read, "Congrats Tiu-Loo! Our favorite thespian!" It had been there since he had returned, and there was no sign of it ever coming down any time soon. As he continued to look at the banner, Professor Hunt appeared from the side of the stage. "Mr. Carter, to what do I owe the pleasure?" he asked. Tiu-Loo pulled a manila folder from his backpack and handed it to the professor.

"I wanted to give this to you. I have a lot of ideas for next year that I think you may like," he said, with a huge smile on his face. Professor Hunt took a brief glance at the papers inside the folder and nodded his head. He was pleased with how well put together and in order Tiu-Loo's presentation was. He had no doubt in his mind that whatever Tiu-Loo had given him, required time and effort. He placed the folder into his large suitcase and walked outside with Tiu-Loo. Before he got into his vehicle, he gave Tiu-Loo some advice. "I want you to stay focused and stay grounded. You've come a long way Mr. Carter, and I'm extremely proud of you," he said. Tiu-Loo thanked him for his kind words and told him to be ready to roll when he returned.

That night, Tiu-Loo decided to sleep over at Holly's place. They had a wonderful evening together. She made dinner, they took a hot bath together, and she gave him a full, body Swedish massage. He had almost fallen asleep, until she told him that they needed to talk. When he heard those words, he knew that it had to be something serious. He sat up on the bed and asked her what it was that they needed to discuss. "I totally forgot that my mom's birthday is this weekend. I have to leave out tomorrow morning," Holly said. It had been a tradition each year for Holly and her family to go to a theme park of her mother's choice each year, to help celebrate her birthday. There was no exception.

"Why are you just now telling me this, Holly?" Tiu-Loo asked, as he looked at her. She tried to tell him that it had slipped her mind. Between the preparations for graduation, her final exams, and trying to spend time with Tiu-Loo, she just never really thought about it. It wasn't until the day before that her mother had called to remind her about the trip. Tiu-Loo wasn't happy. All he wanted to do was hangout with her until it was time for him to head back to Alabama. He tried to be understanding, but the hurt on his face was showing.

Holly gave Tiu-Loo a warm embrace and apologized to him. "I'm so sorry babe. If I could change things, I would. I feel so damn bad for having to leave you," she said. Tiu-Loo told her not to apologize. After all, that was her mother she was talking about, and he would never ask her to choose him over her family at any point in their lives. "I just wanted to have you to myself before you left, that's all," Tiu-Loo said. Holly turned off the lamp that was beside her bed, turned the television off, climbed on top of Tiu-Loo, and started kissing him.

The next morning, Tiu-Loo helped her pack her bags.

He loaded the car for her and checked to make sure she had everything before getting on the highway. "Are you good, babe?" he asked, as he loaded the last piece of luggage into her trunk. "I'm all set, my love," Holly replied. They headed back to campus so that she could drop Tiu-Loo off at his dorm. Once they arrived, she got out and gave him a huge hug. "How about I come visit you in Alabama before you have to depart for the Olympics," she said, as they embraced each other. "That sounds wonderful!" Tiu-Loo replied. He now had something to look forward to soon. "I love you so much, baby," Holly said, while looking into his eyes. She meant every word of it, and Tiu-Loo knew it.

They exchanged a long, deep and passionate kiss before she got back into her car. She looked at Tiu-Loo as if she wanted him to come along with her, but she knew that he couldn't. They were both sad and neither one of them wanted to say goodbye. There never seems to be a right time to say goodbye. "Be safe, baby, and let me know when you make it to your destination," Tiu-Loo said. He told her that he loved her, as he watched her drive off. The next few days were going to be tough for him, but at least he still had Kato around for the moment. They were planning to leave and head back home as soon as the weekend had come. It was Thursday and they were planning to be out of there by Saturday morning.

On Friday afternoon, Tiu-Loo went to the mall with Kato. They bought a few outfits and talked about their plans for the summer. Tiu-Loo already knew that he would have to prepare for the Olympics soon, and Kato was going to be an intern at a therapist's office back home in Alabama. He was excited about the opportunity, because it would give him more expertise in his field of study. He wanted to ultimately become an alcohol and drug abuse counselor. If that didn't work, he wanted to become a therapist for children.

As they sat down in the food court to eat, Tiu-Loo pulled out the flyer that Emilio had given him. He asked Kato if he could look at it for him. As he examined the flyer, he found it strange that his fraternity wanted to have a party for anyone other than one of its members. Of course, they would participate in the occasional charity events, but parties were strictly for one of the frat brothers or to invite ladies over. It also struck Kato as odd that Emilio himself had personally given the flyer to Tiu-Loo. He was well aware of the disdain that he had for him. Kato hadn't been to many gatherings since his argument with Emilio, so he was unaware of this special event of theirs.

"You think I should go?" Tiu-Loo asked Kato. "I don't know, boy-boy. Something just doesn't seem right about this," Kato replied. The party was scheduled to take place that night. He looked at the flyer and had a suggestion. "If you decide to go, just make sure I'm there with you, boy-boy," Kato said, as they finished their meal. Tiu-Loo liked that idea. He figured if the party was being hosted by the fraternity, then nothing crazy could happen if he was there with one of their own. They picked their bags up and proceeded to walk out of the mall.

Kato was talking with Tiu-Loo about the nightly events, when out of nowhere, a young woman approached him. She had been standing by the entrance of the mall. She looked familiar, but Kato couldn't quite put his finger on where he may have known her from. She was a rather tall and curvy individual. She had dark hair, brown eyes, and light-brown skin. Her figure was voluptuous with wide hips. "What's up, sexy? What you got goin?" she asked, as she stuck her tongue out to show off her piercing. Kato smiled and asked what her name was. "I'm Britney," she said, as she walked towards him.

Tiu-Loo stood aside and let Kato talk with her. She asked him if he had any plans later, because she wanted to hang out if he was up for it. "We're going to one of my frat parties tonight. You should come through," Kato said. Britney wasn't feeling it. She wanted to hangout alone with him. "How about you come kick it with me at my place. I promise you won't regret it," she replied, as she continued to flirt with Kato. They exchanged numbers, and Kato told her that he would call her once he had taken Tiu-Loo back to his dorm. She did a seductive walk, as they both said goodbye to each other.

On the way back to campus, Tiu-Loo asked if Kato knew the young lady. He mentioned that she had a familiar face, but he couldn't put two and two together just yet. He didn't think anything of it. Kato always had some girl approaching him. He would go out with a different girl almost every week. Tiu-Loo's phone made a loud beeping sound indicating that the battery was low. "My phone is on 25 percent. I need to charge it," he said. He had been using Kato's extra phone charger for the last two days, because he had misplaced his. He had brought the charger with him to the mall, but Kato's car charger wasn't working. Tiu-Loo made a mental note to grab the charger before he got out of the car.

Once they arrived at Tiu-Loo's dorm, Kato told him that he would meet him at the party. "Wait, you're not coming with me, bro?" Tiu-Loo asked, looking troubled. "I'll meet you at the spot, boy-boy. I'm 'bout to go see what ole girl is talkin' 'bout real quick. I'll be right back," Kato replied, as he assured Tiu-Loo that he wouldn't take long. Kato took off and headed back to his car. "Don't take all day gettin' dressed, boy-boy," Kato said. He pulled off the parking lot, and Tiu-Loo headed to his room. As he looked at his phone, he realized that he had forgotten to get Kato's extra charger from him.

It wasn't a big deal, because he figured Kato would be right back. He texted Holly saying he loved her and let her know that he would be attending the party with Kato later. As it neared time for the beginning of the party, Tiu-Loo still hadn't heard from Kato. His phone had dropped to nearly ten percent, and he was in desperate need of a charger. He called and texted Kato's phone, but he never got a response. Not wanting to constantly call his phone, he left a voicemail for Kato. "Hey bro where you at? I'm 'bout to get ready, so I guess I'll see you there."

The party was going to be at the frat house that was located across the street from campus. Tiu-Loo changed his clothes and got himself ready to head out. While walking across the campus, he noticed that his phone only had five percent of battery life left. He texted Kato and let him know that he would see him at the party soon. He put his phone into his pocket and proceeded to walk up the steps of the frat house.

There was a lot going on. There were many activities taking place outside already. Some of the students were spraying each other with water guns, while others were participating in various drinking games. When Tiu-Loo knocked on the door, he was immediately greeted by Emilio. "Oh shit! You made it. Come on in, man," he said. As Tiu-Loo entered the frat house, Emilio introduced him to everyone. "Hey y'all, show some love to Mr. Olympics right here!" he yelled, as the party goers chanted and clapped their hands. Tiu-Loo felt that he was being sarcastic and quickly went into the living room area of the house. It was like nothing he'd ever seen before. The house was almost packed to capacity.

He looked around to see if he could recognize anyone. Although the flyer mentioned that the other members of the track team would be there, Tiu-Loo hadn't seen anyone yet. While scoping the room, he could see Laziah coming his way. She was smiling from ear to ear, as she worked her way through the crowd. He shook his head as she approached. "Hey handsome, I know you're not still mad at me, are you?"

she asked. "What are you even doing here?" Tiu-Loo asked, starting to become irritated by her presence. Laziah put her hand on Tiu-Loo's shoulder. She wanted to make amends with him. "Look, I'm sorry for the way I acted. There are no hard feelings. Do you accept my apology?" she asked, as she gave Tiu-Loo a playful, sad face.

He tried to act tough, but the face she made was kind of funny to him. "Hey, it's all good. Apology accepted," he replied. They shook hands, and she offered to make him a drink. "There's liquor and punch over there. I can make a cup for you if you'd like," she said politely. Tiu-Loo was a little parched; all the bodies in the party had caused the temperature to rise. "Some punch sounds good. 'Preciate that," he said. She walked over to the punchbowl and grabbed a cup.

As Tiu-Loo waited, Emilio had summoned her to meet him in one of the side bedrooms. He had watched her interact with him the whole time. "So, what's up. He believed you or what?" he asked Laziah. "Hell yea! That shit was too easy, cousin. He was wide open," she replied. Emilio reached in his pockets and handed her four pills. "Here, slip these in his punch. Be fast and don't let nobody see you," he said. He had given her the Mitchell Roddy pills that he purchased from Lil Painty.

Kato had been with Britney for several hours. When he arrived at her house, she had greeted him at the door with nothing but a thong on. Being Kato, he took full advantage of the situation. Her intentions were clear, and he wasn't opposed to them. She cooked for him and they watched a couple of movies. In between the movies, they would pick up where they'd left off in the bedroom. Kato realized that he had been there for a while and told Britney that he was about to leave.

She didn't want him to go. She had been enjoying their time together. "Stay here with me. Emilio and those other dudes don't need you there," she said. Kato quickly stood up. It had finally dawned on him. He hadn't mentioned anything about Emilio to her at all. How would she have known who he was? As he continued to look at her, he realized why her face looked so familiar to him. She was one of the other five girls who had been invited to the party at the barn yard last semester. He knew then that something wasn't right. Tiu-Loo was at that party by himself and he needed to warn him.

He grabbed his keys and phone, and left Britney's house immediately. He could see the many missed calls, texts, and voice message that had been left on his phone. When he tried to call Tiu-Loo, he didn't get an answer. His phone had been dead for a while now. "Muthafucka man!" Kato yelled, as he realized that they were both being set up. He was 35 minutes away from campus, but there was a traffic jam due to an accident that had just taken place. He started to fear for the worst, and he felt that he was probably too late.

Back at the frat house, the party was still going on. Laziah had given the punch to Tiu-Loo and within minutes, he was starting to feel the effects of it. The room was spinning, and he could hardly keep his balance. Seeing that the pills were starting work, Emilio and Laziah took Tiu-Loo upstairs to one of the rooms. "Somebody had a lil too much to drink, I see," Emilio said, as some of the people passed by them on the stairs. Tiu-Loo was barely functioning as they carried him upstairs, but he was totally motionless by the time they had entered the room. When they got Tiu-Loo into the room, Emilio pushed him onto the bed, then helped Laziah take his shoes, shirt, and pants off. The Mitchell Roddy pills were extremely powerful.

Once his clothes were off, Emilio handed Laziah a large, tube sock that had three big bars of soap in it. "You know what to do," he said to her. She nodded her head, and he walked out of the room. Laziah stood next to one of the mirrors in the bedroom and smiled, as she looked at herself. She wrapped the top of the sock around her fist, leaving just enough length for it to hang. Suddenly, she began hitting herself in the face. Her face turned red, as she continued to wail away with each hit. Finally, after a few more solid licks, her lips were busted, and her eye had become black.

She put the sock down and took off her top shirt. She had on a tank top and mini skirt. She balled the front of her tank top up and then used her hands to rip it down the middle. She then purposely ripped her panties and pulled them down, close to her knees, carefully walked over to the bed, and laid next to Tiu-Loo. As he lay stretched out, Laziah hovered over him and looked at his body. She rubbed on his chest, legs, and arms. Tiu-Loo had slowly started coming to, but she didn't realize it. With no regards to his physical state, she slowly started to fondle his genitals.

As she played with his manhood, Tiu-Loo's eyes began to open. He couldn't tell what was going on, and his vision was blurry. He felt someone touching him, but he was still trying to gather himself. His eyes felt heavy, and his legs were numb. He wiggled his toes and fingers; everything seemed to work fine, but he still felt like he was paralyzed. When he looked down, he could see Laziah's head resting on his stomach. He mustered up just enough energy to sit himself up. "Yo, what the fuck you doin?!" he asked, as he tried to get the sensation back into his legs. Laziah was startled. She didn't think Tiu-Loo would be up so fast. The pills were supposed to knock him out for several hours, but Tiu-Loo had managed to wake up after the first hour had passed.

He looked around and saw that his clothes had been taken off. He was furious about the fact that he didn't know how or why he was in a random room at the party. "Where the hell are my clothes!?" Tiu-Loo screamed, as he was starting to become enraged. Seeing that he was starting to make it to his feet, Laziah screamed for help. "Somebody please, help me! He's going crazy!" she yelled. She forced tears to come out of her eyes, screaming and crying hysterically. Standing right outside the door was Emilio. He called two of his frat brothers upstairs, and they rushed into the room to help Laziah.

When Emilio saw that Tiu-Loo had woken up, he too was surprised. Not wanting to break character, Emilio and his two frat brothers rushed Tiu-Loo. They grabbed him and held him down. His body was so weak from the pills, that he didn't have the energy to try and fight them off. "Your sick ass tryin to rape my lil cousin, huh? Somebody, call the cops right now!" Emilio said. Tiu-Loo was lost. He had no idea Laziah and Emilio were related. He had no recollection of how he ended up in the room with her, either. All he knew was that he'd taken a sip out of a cup that was given to him, and now, there were three guys holding him against his will.

Tiu-Loo tried to plead his case, but no one was trying to listen to him. "I don't know what the hell is going on! I didn't put my hands on that girl!" he said. When he saw the blood on Laziah's lips and the blackened eye, he knew that something terrible had occurred. He tried to free himself, but there was no way he was going to get out of their clutches. As he continued to struggle, the other members of the party entered the room. They couldn't believe what they were witnessing. One of the young ladies had offered her jacket to Laziah after seeing that her tank top had been ripped. She asked Laziah what happened, and she replied, "He tried to rape me!"

The cops finally came and rushed upstairs to the bedroom. Once they reached Laziah, they listened to her give her account of the events that had taken place. "He slapped me and punched me. He told me that if I wouldn't give it to him, then he was gonna take it," she said, as she cried even harder. Emilio ran over to Laziah to console her. As he hugged her, he whispered in her ear, "You're doing good. We finally got his ass." Tiu-Loo pleaded with the cops to let him go. "Please officer, I don't know what happened. I'm an Olympic athlete. I wouldn't jeopardize that!" he yelled, but they didn't want to hear what he had to say. A young lady had a busted lip, and ripped clothes, and Tiu-Loo had no pants or shirt on his body. They had no choice but to believe what they had seen, and what they had been told. Tiu-Loo was going to jail.

Kato had finally made it through traffic. He had been stuck for nearly two hours. When he made it to the frat house, the cops were already taking Tiu-Loo to one of the squad cars. He stopped in the middle of the street and rushed over to see what the problem was. "Tiu-Loo, what the hell happened?! Are you okay?" he asked. "Back up, son! This is official police business," one of the cops stated. As they loaded Tiu-Loo into the car, he asked Kato to do him a favor. "Bro, call my uncle and Holly. Let them know what's going on. They're taking me downtown now," he said. Kato was heartbroken. His best friend was about to go to jail, and he felt it was all his fault. He wasn't there when he needed him, and he blamed himself. As the police cruiser drove off, Tiu-Loo looked at Kato. He wasn't mad, but he was definitely gripped with fear.

Tears filled Kato's eyes as he watched Tiu-Loo get taken

away. There's no way he could've been guilty of whatever they were accusing him of. One thing he was certain of, was that Emilio had to be behind it. He balled his fists and went straight into the frat house. Once he made it inside, he immediately confronted Emilio. "Yo, what the hell happened in here?" he asked. Emilio smirked as he answered Kato's question. "Why don't you ask your raping ass friend," he replied. Kato didn't believe him for one second. He listened to Emilio explain what happened in the bedroom. As he continued to talk, Laziah appeared beside him with one of the female police officers. She was about to head to the hospital to be examined.

When Kato saw her face, he was caught off guard. It was unbelievable to see the bruises and injuries that she had acquired. He felt sorry for her, but he didn't think Tiu-Loo was responsible for her face looking the way that it did. "Man, y'all can miss me with that shit. Ain't no way Tiu-Loo did that to her!" Kato said. "Well, my lil cousin wouldn't lie. She's a good girl, homie," Emilio said. The female officer escorted Laziah to the ambulance that was waiting outside for her. As Kato recognized her face, he made a startling revelation. "Yea, well yo lil good, girl cousin is a freak. No one has to take a thing from her hot ass," he said.

Before he could finish his sentence, Emilio had rushed over to Kato. He swung and missed. That would be a costly mistake, because as Kato dodged his punch, he countered with a vicious right hook to Emilio's jaw and nearly broke it. Perry and the other frat brothers quickly broke the fight up.

They tried to calm the two of them down, because they didn't want to see either one of them go to jail that night. Passions were high, which meant that an eventual altercation was inevitable. "And if I find out you had anything to do with this, ima fuck you up some more!" Kato said, as he left the house. Emilio spit out the blood that had filled his mouth.

The next morning, Kato made the phone call to Holly and Uncle Kobe. His bags were packed, but he still hadn't put them into his car. He was worried about Tiu-Loo. They were supposed to head back home together to relax and enjoy the summer, but that thought had been destroyed. He turned the television on, and there was a breaking story appearing on the local news. "Track and Field star Chase Carter, also known as Tiu-Loo, is now in police custody. He's being charged with sexual assault, attempted rape, and aggravated, first degree battery. He was slated to be on the U.S. Olympic team in August, but that will not happen. He's being held on 250 thousand dollars bond," the news reporter announced. Kato turned the television off and dropped his head. It was about to be an extremely long and cruel summer.

Chapter 9: Operation Gator

His knuckles were hardened from punching on the concrete floor each day. He had lost a considerable amount of weight, due to his refusal to eat the food that was being served in prison. The last few nights had been lonely and miserable. Tiu-Loo was having trouble coping with the loss of his beloved Uncle Kobe. It had been two years since the judge had sentenced him to serve time at a maximum-security prison. After being found guilty on two of the three charges, a Florida judge sentenced Tiu-Loo to 10 years in prison. As Uncle Kobe walked out of the courtroom, he suffered a massive heart attack. By the time he was rushed to the hospital, he was pronounced dead on arrival.

This was Tiu-Loo's second time being sent to the hole. Solitary confinement had become the norm for him. This time, he was told that he had to stay in for 90 days. It didn't bother him. He ate just enough food to have the energy that he needed to exercise. He was given a new book to read every week, which helped his time in the hole go by a little faster. He went into prison with a different mentality; kill or be killed was the only mind frame that he could adapt to. He had been involved in several fights and he was open to participating in many more.

His last fight nearly cost him his freedom. One of the

inmates caught wind of the charges he had been convicted of and decided that he would confront Tiu-Loo. When Tiu-Loo was in the chow line, the inmate charged at him with a homemade shank. As they tussled and wrestled, Tiu-Loo ended up stabbing him with his own weapon. Had the blade gone an inch deeper, the inmate would've died. Tiu-Loo didn't look for trouble, but he certainly wasn't the one to be messed with. He was going to protect himself at all times, even if it meant dying in the process.

Luckily, there were cameras in the Chow Hall. After concluding the investigation, the warden of the prison found that Tiu-Loo wasn't the aggressor in that instance. He could've been given an extra fifteen years or sentenced to life had he been found to be at fault. Instead, they opted for the 90-day confinement and hoped that Tiu-Loo would stay out of trouble. His world had been turned upside down since being wrongfully convicted. No matter what people thought of the situation, Tiu-Loo maintained his innocence.

As he spent his time in the hole, he could hear the sounds of the other inmates on the floor. Some of them had been in prison for decades. One of the inmates next door to him had been in prison for nearly 30 years. He was a child molester and was said to have molested hundreds of children. Mr. Fogelman had been an elementary school teacher for many years. He would host private study sessions at his home with permission from his students' parents. After the sessions, he would invite one of the students to the basement for ice cream. Once they were in the basement, Mr. Fogelman would do unspeakable things to them. He was given a life sentence after prosecutors produced mountains of evidence against him.

He was given the option of protective custody, but he refused it. He didn't think the inmates would attack an aging 58-year-old white man. He couldn't have been more wrong. Mr. Fogelman had forgotten one of the golden rules in prison. Whatever you do to little children, in turn, would be executed and done to you. That was the street law. Needless to say, he had it very tough throughout his prison stints. He had previously been transferred to three different prisons, because of the many assaults that he had endured. After a while, he would purposely keep illegal contraband in his cell, in order to get away from the general population. Each day, he would sing the alphabet song to himself before eating. It was a ritual that Tiu-Loo saw as extremely weird and bizarre.

Other inmates would yell loudly at the guards or beat on the walls inside their cells. Tiu-Loo did his best to weed out the distractions. He had learned different techniques on how to strengthen his body from watching old martial arts videos with Uncle Kobe. He punched the concrete every day to strengthen and numb his knuckles, while executing 300 pushups and sit-ups as his daily regimen. The food had been another story. Very seldom would he eat everything on his tray. If there was bread or fruit, Tiu-Loo would eat that with no issue. Anything else would be given away to another inmate in exchange for candy or another piece of food. Thankfully, he still had Kato, who would put money on his books whenever he could. That money allowed Tiu-Loo to get commissary, which helped him attain the essential items that he needed such as hygiene products.

He had completed his 90 days, and it was time to return to his cell block. There were inmates locked up for several reasons, ranging from kidnapping to murder. As the guards escorted Tiu-Loo to his cell, he could see that a lot had changed in his three-month absence. It wasn't uncommon for new inmates to come and go, but he was in a totally new atmosphere. He had been switched from his original downstairs block to a new one up top. His old cell mate had been sent to the infirmary, because someone had put small pieces of glass into his bowl of chili. He was known to be a snitch, and someone sought after revenge for ratting.

Once he made it to his new cell, the guards removed the chains that were around his legs. When he walked in, he could see that a cellmate had already been occupying the space. He had a low haircut and what looked like white skin, but with a sun tan. He had tattoos on his forearms and spoke English and Spanish. Tiu-Loo was familiar with the Spanish that he was taught in high school, but this man spoke it a little differently. He stood about 5 feet and 10 inches, with a lean, slim build. His brown eyes were relaxed; they always seemed to be set and focused.

"Asere que bola?" the man said, as he tried to greet Tiu-Loo. His sudden moves caused Tiu-Loo to get into a defensive stance. "Bro, I'll fuck you up if you get any closer!" he said, as he squared up to anticipate the man's next move. "Eres un punto," he said, laughing at Tiu-Loo. He extended his hand and introduced himself. "Relax asere. I'm Alvaro, but you can call me Gator. Believe me, I don't want any more trouble than you do," he said. Once he realized that everything was cool, Tiu-Loo was finally able to let his guards down. Prison was an unpredictable environment, and you could never get too comfortable with anyone inside. Tiu-Loo shook his hand and told him his name as well.

Tiu-Loo was very guarded because of the charges that were pinned against him. He assumed that everyone was either trying to hurt him or get next to him in an effort to cause him harm. Rape and child molestation were serious offenses in prison and were greatly frowned upon. Whenever Tiu-Loo would encounter a new cellmate, he would promptly tell them the reason why he was in prison. Most of them would understand because they may have been in there for the same reasons. However, a couple didn't like the fact that they were cellmates with a potential rapist. Consequently, this would cause a fight or three to ensue. Tiu-Loo always held his own. He was a scrappy fighter and had learned quite a few moves from his sparring sessions with his late, Uncle Kobe.

Once Tiu-Loo got his bunk together, he began explaining his conviction and charges to Gator. "No worries, asere. I already know about you," he said. Seeing that Gator still hadn't made any suspicious moves, Tiu-Loo wondered what was up with him. Before he had been transferred to the cell, Gator and a few inmates had what was known as a paperwork party. It was a gathering where they would get information by looking up the booking number and case of a fellow inmate. Initially, Gator thought that he would be in a cell with a sick and twisted individual. Moreover, he knew that once he met him, he was going to cause a great deal of harm to him.

However, once he looked up Tiu-Loo's story in the prison library, he found it to be unique. He admired the fact that Tiu-Loo had accomplished so much while he was in college. After Gator had gone over the facts of the case, he found that there were a lot of inconsistencies. Many of the instances just didn't add up, and he knew without a shadow of a doubt that Tiu-Loo was innocent. If anything, he wanted Tiu-Loo to know that he was on his side. Gator knew that prison was an unfortunate hell hole, and no human being should ever be forced to endure solitary confinement. You would literally lose your mind in there.

Tiu-Loo was fascinated by how smart Gator was. He wanted to know what Gator had been saying when he was introducing himself; his Spanish was different, but he was intrigued by it. "Well, I'm from Cuba. Asere means like dude or brother, and eres un punto means you're weird," Gator said, as he continued to converse with Tiu-Loo. He listened carefully as Gator went into a few vocabulary words in Cuban Spanish. He was curious to know how someone as bright as Gator could've ended up in prison. As Gator continued to talk, Tiu-Loo finally asked him the question. "So, if you don't mind me asking, what are you locked up for?"

Gator had an entirely different background growing up. He had no problem inviting Tiu-Loo into his world. In many ways, talking about his past became a form of therapy for him. Alvaro Perez was born and raised in Cuba. At the age of fourteen, he and his family had relocated and moved to Miami, Florida. His father promised that he would meet up with the family once he had earned enough money while working, but he never showed up. He met a younger woman and started another family with her.

Now being forced to be the man of the house, Gator ran the streets with a local gang to help put food on the table. He had to help feed his mother and younger sister by any means. By the age of 21, he had amassed a fortune. After a few successful bank robberies and overthrowing most of the local drug dealers in the city, Gator had become a legend in the streets of Miami. However, his days of being a street boss would come to an end a few short years later. At the age of 25, he was sentenced to 10 years in prison for running a robbery ring that expanded across seven different states. He would've been given more time, but prosecutors couldn't compete with his expensive lawyers.

Tiu-Loo was in awe of the stories that Gator was telling him. At first glance, you wouldn't think that Gator would be capable of such things. Once he looked at the intensity in his eyes as he went down memory lane, Tiu-Loo could tell that he meant business. As he accumulated so much wealth, Gator hid some of his money. Once the coast was clear, he had his sister, Esmerelda, move back to Cuba to open a few legit businesses. His plan was to go back once he was released from prison. "Yea, I love my little sister. She's smart and she's loyal," Gator said, as he continued to discuss his plans for the future.

He had done his time gracefully. He didn't complain; he held himself accountable and accepted his fate like a man. Tiu-Loo wished that he had that same bearing about himself, but he just couldn't. Trying to keep a positive outlook on his situation had become very difficult. There were many men who deserved to be in prison for the things they had done, but he knew that he was innocent. The only way he could cope with things was by making a weekly phone call to Holly or Kato. He only had about fifteen minutes to talk each time, so he would make the most of it with them. Usually, he would call Kato who would then make a three-way phone call to Holly.

Gator had been waiting patiently for his release. He had three more months to go, and he was excited about getting out. "I swear, once I get out, I'm gonna eat a huge bowl of Ropa Vieja," he said, as he rubbed his stomach. Gator was referring to the Cuban meal that consisted of shredded beef that is cooked in tomatoes and served over fluffy white rice. The term literally translated to "old cloths," because leftovers could be stored into the recipe easily. The way

Gator was explaining the taste to Tiu-Loo, made him crave it as well. He could tell that Gator loved his family. He had pictures of his family on the wall of his bunk.

There was one picture that caught Tiu-Loo's attention. The woman had long hair with blue eyes. Her skin matched that of Gator's but had more of a smooth texture. She was wearing a bathing suit and was on the beach with another young lady. She was striking a pose as if she had been preparing for a photoshoot. Her beauty was stunning. "So, who is this?" Tiu-Loo asked, as he pointed to the picture. "Oh, that's my hermana, Esmerelda," Gator replied. He could tell that Tiu-Loo was stricken by how gorgeous she was. "Maybe I can introduce you to her one year," Gator said. Tiu-Loo laughed it off. "I doubt that will ever happen. I've never even been outside of the country," he replied.

Tiu-Loo hopped up into his bunk and looked at the ceiling. He had a hard time sleeping in the hole, and he spent the last of his energy conversing with Gator. Before he could close his eyes, Gator got his attention once more. "Hey, they're letting us go to the library next week. I can show you a few books to read and we can look into your case more," he said, as he returned to his bunk. Tiu-Loo didn't say anything. He was sound asleep in minutes. It was 3 p.m. when he fell asleep, and he didn't wake up until the next morning.

When they made it to the library the following week, Gator gave Tiu-Loo a few books to read. They were highly informative and talked about many different subjects. One was written by a forensics expert that talked about how people got away with murder. Another book talked about civil rights activists, and the many obstacles they faced during the Jim Crow era. As soon as Tiu-Loo received the books from Gator, he immediately sat down and started reading them. He found that the book about getting away with murder had been interesting. Many of the serial killers were smart. They just seem to have been triggered by something traumatic in their lives.

As Tiu-Loo read his book, Gator was hiding in one of the corners of the library. He had a cellphone that had been snuck into the facility by one of the prison guards. It was easy to have certain things provided if your money was right. He didn't have the phone to have fun and chat. For years, Gator had been secretly helping other inmates fight their case from inside the prison walls that confined them. He only helped if he felt that the individual was truly not guilty of the crime. He would look up their cases and help them file an appeal based on the facts and evidence. He had only helped a few others, but in every instance, they were retried, and ultimately found not guilty.

To him, Tiu-Loo's case had a million holes in the story. An Olympic hopeful attempting to rape a girl at a packed house party just didn't seem like it made sense. He had no history of doing drugs, but miraculously, there were pills found in his system. When he woke up, he was completely unaware of what happened. Even with those facts, Gator would've believed that it was possible to commit a crime of that magnitude. However, when he heard that there was no semen or fingerprints discovered from Tiu-Loo on or around the alleged victim's body, he knew that something wasn't right. Whomever was behind setting him up, had been very clever at planning the events leading up to that fateful night. Being an actual criminal, Gator knew that prison was no place for any innocent person. If he could find a way to help others, then he would do just that.

When he went over to the table where Tiu-loo was sitting, he pulled out the phone to show him what he had been up to. "Yo, what are you doing, bro? You trying to get us put in the hole?" Tiu-Loo whispered. He cautiously looked around to see if any guards were present. "We're gonna get you out of here, one way or another," Gator said. He explained to Tiu-Loo that he could help him if he wanted him to, but it was his choice. After breaking down a few of the discrepancies that he had discovered, Tiu-Loo was surprised. He had never really studied his case after he was convicted. He had been tired of fighting, and his spirit was broken. Although he was happy that Gator had found the new material, Tiu-Loo declined his offer. He was exhausted and didn't think the hassle was worth it.

Gator advised him to call one of his closest friends or relatives. He felt that Tiu-Loo would have a great chance of exoneration, if he had his case retried. Tiu-Loo thanked Gator for his efforts but didn't want to talk about the case anymore. He got up from the table, grabbed his books, and proceeded to walk out of the library. He had mixed emotions about his predicament. One minute, he was cool with just doing his time but on the other hand, he understood that he wasn't guilty and wanted to be released from prison as soon as possible.

As Tiu-Loo walked back to his cell, one of the inmates called out to him. "Hey bitch! Don't let me catch you slippin! Ima fuck you up when I see you!" he said. It was Snooty. He had a vendetta against Tiu-Loo because he believed the story that had been told about him. He figured he was given a light sentence, and he wanted to make an example out of him. Snooty was a known gang banger from California. By the time he was seventeen, he had been in and out of juvenile detention homes on numerous occasions. He was serving a fifteen-year bid for manslaughter. Trained as an MMA fighter, he had brutal power in his kicks and punches. Before his 27th birthday, he had gotten into an argument with a couple of bouncers at a night club. After a heated argument, the 6'2, 225- pound Snooty exchanged blows with them both.

When it was all over, one of the bouncers was dead, while the other one had been sent to the hospital in critical condition. During his trial, the judge showed no mercy after Snooty stated that he wished the other bouncer would've died as well. He quickly became one of the enforcers in the prison. Consequently, this led to him being on lockdown or in the hole, most of the time. He would beat people up if they were in debt and had even been said to be known as a "booty goon." This meant that he had a very thuggish persona, but he also liked men as well.

Tiu-Loo laughed at Snooty as he walked by. Snooty continued to shake the door of his cell, while threatening Tiu-Loo. "You just wait, fuck boy!" Snooty continued on. "Yea, okay, girlfriend. You got it, sweetheart," Tiu-Loo taunted, as the other inmates laughed uncontrollably. Even the guards found his rapid response to be a bit comical. They had grown tired of his constant threats to individuals, day in and day out. He was always instigating or in the middle of unnecessary drama.

When Tiu-Loo made it back to his cell, one of the guards came to let him know that he had a visitor. He didn't know who it could've been. Holly refused to visit him, and Kato hadn't been to the prison in over a year. As the guard led Tiu-Loo to the visitation room, he wondered who could possibly be there to see him. Once they made it to the visitation area, he was overcome with joy and emotion. Coach Cameron and Professor Hunt had made the nearly six-hour drive to the country part of Florida to visit Tiu-Loo.

They sat down and started to catch up on the good times. Professor Hunt shared with Tiu-Loo the good news about the play that he had written two years prior. He told him that most of the proceeds were donated to a fund that had been created in his honor. The students had performed the play and it had been the best production by far. The money that the theatre students raised, had been put into a bank account for Tiu-Loo to have access to whenever he was to be released from prison. Professor Hunt was happy to see his old student.

Coach Cameron was observing Tiu-Loo's demeanor. He knew that it had been a while since he had seen anyone that was close to him. He tried to imagine the things that Tiu-Loo may have had to experience while he did his time. These thoughts made him feel even more sympathy for Tiu-Loo. As Tiu-Loo continued to talk with Professor Hunt, he realized that Coach Cameron still hadn't said anything. "Yo, what's up, Coach? Snap out of it," he said jokingly. He could tell that Coach Cameron had been in deep thought. He also knew that he didn't want to tell him about the outcome of the Olympics.

Because Tiu-Loo had forfeited his spot on the team, due to his conviction, Emilio was able to take his spot. He had an incredible run at the Olympic Games. He made it to the finals of the long jump, where he earned a silver medal. He graduated with his bachelor's degree in education and became a teacher back in his hometown of Miami. He called Coach Cameron a week before his visit to see Tiu-Loo. He was inviting him to his wedding, and he wanted him to meet his two-year old son.

Tiu-Loo had already been aware of the Olympics. He was mad at first, but he eventually got over it. There was nothing he could do about it anyway. As they were about to conclude their visit, Professor Hunt told Tiu-Loo the real reason for their visit. "We've been studying your case and have retained a lawyer to take a second look for you," he said. Coach Cameron nodded his head, as he saw that Tiu-Loo was in disbelief. It was a surreal feeling because Gator was just talking to him about this same thing. Hearing Professor Hunt say those words, gave Tiu-Loo a sense of hope.

"Now, it may take a little time, but we believe that we can get you out of here within a year or two," Coach Cameron said, as he explained the process. Tiu-Loo hugged them both. He still didn't believe that he would be able to leave prison anytime soon, but their words made him hopeful. They said their goodbyes and encouraged Tiu-Loo to keep his head held high. Brighter days would come after the storm, and Tiu-Loo would soon have his moment of glory. While seeing his old teacher and coach had eased his mind for a moment, the harsh realities of prison were nearly inescapable.

Tiu-Loo and Gator had formed a strong and unbreakable bond. He would teach Tiu-Loo his Cuban Spanish, and Tiu-Loo would break down the mechanics of track and field to him every now and then. Each morning, they would get a deck of cards and do pushups and sit ups, until the deck was completed. They were always around each other, and one day, their loyalty to one another was going to be tested.

A couple of months had passed, and the Florida

summer had been unmerciful; like, shoot you in your face and make it reversable. The prison's air conditioning unit decided to stop working. This caused a record 21 deaths within a span of weeks. In order to gain control of his prison, the warden ordered the guards to let the inmates go out for their rec time at least twice a day. The change of rules helped a little but was still potentially dangerous. Many rival gang members and natural enemies would be in closer proximity with each other, which meant that a riot could ensue at any moment.

The day had come for Tiu-Loo's block to go outside for their rec time. The guards felt that it was okay to keep the other inmates outside, because there hadn't been any issues in the last few weeks. When they made it to the yard, the basketball court was full. Nearly all the inmates were playing a game or waiting their turn for one. Tiu-Loo and Gator chose to go lift weights instead. There was a weight bench with several free weights of different sizes nearby. As they headed over to prep for their workout, one of Gator's old friends called him over to the basketball court to have a talk with him.

He told Tiu-Loo to go ahead and start and that he would be back momentarily. He ran across the yard to greet his friend. As he walked away from Tiu-Loo, Snooty went over to confront him. He had been watching them since the moment they had stepped foot outside. He remembered how slick Tiu-Loo had been with him, and he wanted to see if he was really about that life. Tiu-Loo had been doing a set of arm curls when he was suddenly approached by Snooty. "What's up, fuck boy. Talk that shit now, homie!" he said, as one of his other partners was standing beside him. Tiu-Loo dropped the weights and stared at Snooty.

He could see that Snooty had a shank in his hand. "Yea, I'm 'bout to fuck you up," Snooty said, as his partner peeped the scene to see if the guards were on alert. "What? I'm supposed be scared 'cause you got a shank on you, honey bun?" Tiu-Loo asked sarcastically. That grinded Snooty's gears. Before he could raise the shank in his hands, Tiu-Loo had already socked Snooty in his mouth. The hit instantly dropped Snooty to his knees, as he spit one of his teeth out. The shank had been dislodged from his hand and had fallen on the ground. Tiu-Loo jumped on top of him and began punching him in his face. Snooty's partner didn't waste time. He tackled Tiu-Loo and began fighting with him as well.

As Snooty began to stand to his feet, he spotted the shank and grabbed it. Tiu-Loo was preoccupied with his partner, so he didn't see him coming. Gator saw the commotion, and he could see that Tiu-Loo was in danger. "Me Piro!" he said to his friend, as he ran as fast as he could across the yard. Tiu-Loo was still fighting when Snooty snuck up behind him with the shank. He drew back his hand with the intent to stab Tiu-Loo in his back, but he was swiftly knocked off his feet and unconscious. Gator had grabbed one of the ten-pound metal plates and cracked Snooty across the head with it.

By this time, the prison guards had seen the fight unfold. However, they turned their heads and looked in the opposite direction as if nothing happened. They were tired of seeing Snooty bully other people. They appeared relieved about him being knocked out. As Tiu-Loo fought Snooty's partner, Gator grabbed the shank. He stuck the blade in his leg, twisting it at the same time. The man let out a sound that sounded like a wounded animal. "Ahhhh Shit! My leg!" he screamed in agony. "Yea Bitch!" Tiu-Loo yelled, as he gave him one final kick to the face.

By now, the guards had made it over to the scene. As gratifying as it was to see Snooty laid out on the ground, they still had to do their jobs. "Alright, y'all come with me," one of the guards said. He was one of the head correctional officers on the shift. Mr. Chalmers was a seasoned vet. He had been a prison guard for over 20 years and had known Gator for eight of them. As he escorted them back to their cell, he reminded Gator to keep his eye on the prize. "Come on, Gator, you leave in two days. Don't mess that up, man," he said. "Asere, I know that, but there was no way in hell I was gonna let them kill my brother," Gator replied. Mr. Chalmers could do nothing but respect what Gator said.

They made it back to their cell, and Tiu-Loo immediately apologized. "My bad, bro. I didn't mean to get you involved in that shit," he said. "Say nothing more of it. We're brothers. I got you," Gator replied. They had experienced a lot in such a short amount of time. Gator had a bag of chips and some candy bars tucked away in his stash. He pulled out a bag and handed it to Tiu-Loo. "Now, show me how you threw that first punch," Gator requested. Tiu-Loo stood up and gave a demonstration. "Esta valoa!" Gator said, as he took a bite of his candy bar.

The day had come for Gator's release. He made his bunk for the last time, and he had given all his unwanted items to Tiu-Loo. Many of the other inmates chanted his name, as he prepared to leave. They had given him a mini going away celebration the night before. Mr. Chalmers even snuck in a small beer for him to drink that night. He was ready to leave, but still wished that Tiu-Loo didn't have to waste his time away sitting in that cell. They had created memories that would last forever, and Gator was more than honored to have known Tiu-Loo.

"You get out of here and make something of yourself," Gator said, as he embraced Tiu-Loo. They shook hands and waited for the guard to open the door of their cell. As he waited to be officially released, one of the guards on duty delivered an envelope to Tiu-Loo. "Bout time, man, finally!" he said, as he read the name on the letter. It was a letter from Holly. He hadn't heard from her much, because of her scheduling conflict at work. She was working doubles as a nurse. They would still talk on the phone when he would call Kato, but she hadn't written him as much as she used to. He had a huge smile on his face when he saw that it came from her.

"See, you're already starting the day off right," Gator

said. He was about to open the letter and read it, but the supervising guard had come to let Gator out of the cell. "Alright, Perez, it's time to go," he said. Gator quickly grabbed a pin. He wrote down his email, his phone number, and his sister's phone number. "I don't think you'll be in here much longer. You call me whenever you need me, my brother. Chao pescao!" he said, as he shook Tiu-Loo's hand one last time. "Dale!" Tiu-Loo responded. Gator was gone within seconds, and just like that, the cell was quiet again.

Tiu-Loo thought about the talks they had, and what Gator had taught him. He knew that he would never meet a person as genuine and trustworthy as Gator again. There were things they discussed that Tiu-Loo had never revealed before. For example, he always felt that Emilio had set him up, but he just never had the ocular proof that he did. Gator once had a handsome son. He had the same name and looked just like him, but he was killed when one of his enemies shot his house up while executing a drive by. It was retaliation for one of the many robberies that Gator had committed. His son was only three years old. Sometimes at night, Tiu-Loo could hear Gator talking in his sleep. It was as if he had nightmares about it constantly. He felt so sorry for him. He couldn't imagine what it may have felt like to lose a child, but it seemed to be a painful experience.

He sat down to read the letter that Holly had written him. He was so excited; he always looked forward to reading her kind words that were so well thought out, and full of wisdom and strength. As he opened the letter, he saw that there was only one sheet of paper that was folded. He shook the envelope, held it upside down, and looked inside of it to see if there could've possibly been a sheet that he had missed. He had never seen a single sheet of paper in a letter from Holly. Her letters were always three pages or more.

He unfolded the sheet of paper. It was short and straight to the point. "Dear Chase, I truly do love you, but I simply can't do this anymore. I wish you good health and prosperity, but I think we should both move on. Please take care of yourself. Love you," the letter said. Tiu-Loo said nothing. He folded the paper and put it back into the envelope. The woman that he thought he could possibly spend the rest of his life with, had just broken up with him. By the time he was done punching the walls, he had nearly broken through the concrete barrier.

Chapter 10: Success!

"After a thorough investigation, and new findings within our department, we have concluded that one, Mr. Chase Marley Carter, is not responsible for the alleged incident that occurred four years ago. The state asks that he be released to his family immediately and we offer a public apology for him and his loved ones as well," said the state prosecutor, as she read her final statement to the judge. After four years, four months, and four days, Tiu-Loo was finally a free man. His lawyer, Ms. Susan Gorman, had worked tirelessly on his new case. The 5'5" blonde hair and blue-eyed woman was the definition of a pit bull in a skirt.

She had studied law for nearly eight years, before co-founding an organization with a fellow business partner. "Wake Up Doc" was an organization that focused on proving the innocence of convicted rapists and murderers with the use of DNA evidence. After being referred to her, Coach Cameron contacted Ms. Gorman to see if there was anything they could do about Tiu-Loo's case. Seeing that Coach Cameron was serious about getting justice for Tiu-Loo, Professor Hunt offered to help pay for his legal expenses.

Ms. Gorman carefully went over the facts of the case. As her team investigated, they interviewed several witnesses from the party four years ago. Two of them said that Tiu-Loo's body was limp and lifeless, and that he had been helped to the upstairs room. If he couldn't walk up the stairs by himself, then it was impossible for him to be able to physically assault anyone. Also, it was revealed that the very people who'd helped him gain access to the room, were also the last ones to be seen with Tiu-Loo before the incident.

By the end of the investigation, it had been determined that not only had Tiu-Loo been unconscious for a significant amount of time, but that he could've possibly been set up as well. There was absolutely no exchange of bodily fluids found whatsoever. The DNA evidence was way too strong to overlook. Although it had taken a few years, Tiu-Loo was happy to be returning home. The judge apologized to Tiu-Loo as well. He promised that he would have his record wiped clean immediately following the proceedings.

Tiu-Loo stood up and hugged Ms. Gorman. Her unselfish and extensive work had been greatly appreciated. For the first time in four long years, Tiu-Loo could finally breathe a sigh of relief. He had nearly turned into a complete savage in prison. He actually planned to kill Snooty if he had approached him again. He knew that the beef between them would never end until one of them was six feet under the ground. Tiu-Loo had made a shank and was ready for the day to come. Thankfully a couple of days before carrying out his plan, a prison guard was at his cell telling him to prepare for court.

As he walked outside of the courtroom, Tiu-Loo was met by a host of people. Coach Cameron, Professor Hunt, and Kato had been listening to the proceedings while waiting outside. The judge didn't want any distractions in his courtroom, so he asked that no one be present, other than Tiu-Loo's defense team. When he saw Kato, they embraced each other at once. "Wassup, boy-boy! I'm so glad you're free!" Kato said, as he continued to hug Tiu-Loo. "Feels good, fa sho!" Tiu-Loo replied. Coach Cameron and Professor Hunt joined in, creating a group hug. They all rejoiced with Tiu-Loo as they understood the journey he had been on to clear his name.

Due to it being such a high-profile case, there were tons of reporters and television outlets waiting in the halls of the courtroom. Before Tiu-Loo could officially walk into the world of freedom, a news reporter approached him to conduct a brief interview. "Mr. Carter, now that you've been released, what do you plan to do?" she asked. He took a second to think, and then he replied. "I just plan to live, that's all." The reporter wasn't satisfied with that answer. She wanted Tiu-Loo to go into detail about what he meant. "Could you be a little more specific? I don't quite understand what you mean," she said. "See, that's the thing. The hardest thing about the business, is simply minding your own," Tiu-Loo replied. The news reporter's mouth was wide open. If ever there had been a state of shock, she was surely a first-class resident.

Tiu-Loo walked outside and stood on the steps. He took

a deep breath and let it all sink in. He continued to look around him, as if reality hadn't kicked in yet. He wanted to make sure that he wasn't dreaming and that some officer was going to tell him to turn around and go back inside. His long dreadlocks had been pinned up in a manbun for a month. He removed his rubber band and let his hair down. At that moment, he knew that he was officially a free man.

There were news reporters standing on the opposite side of the street. Tiu-Loo really wasn't in the mood to talk with anyone else. "Hey Mr. Carter, you got a second?" the heavy-set man asked, as he attempted to run over to where Tiu-Loo was standing. Kato saw that the reporter was trying to cross the street. "Hey, can you still run, boy-boy?" Kato asked. "Hell yea, you better know it bro," Tiu-Loo replied. "Well, the car is this way," Kato said, as he pointed in a direction located a few blocks down. They took off running, while they laughed at the reporter trying to catch up. It was funny seeing him trying to dodge the cars, as he ran in the middle of the street.

Once they made it to Kato's car, they got in and waited to hear from Coach Cameron and Professor Hunt. However, they had already gotten on the highway and were heading home. "We need to take you to get a shape up, boy-boy," Kato said. Indeed, Tiu-Loo had been in desperate need of one. He wasn't allowed to have a razor while he was in prison. He would usually get a line-up by one of the barbers on his cell block, but for the last three months, he had been busy reading law books in the library.

It was a warm November afternoon, and Thanksgiving was roughly three weeks away. As Kato drove, he asked Tiu-Loo if he was hungry. "Man, I want a huge burger, some fries, and a large chocolate milkshake!" Tiu-Loo said. He had been craving a milkshake for years. He would have at least one per week after he had finished with track practice. Kato liked the sound of that as well. He himself had worked up an appetite after they ran away from the news reporter.

They ended up going to a burger spot not too far from the courthouse. A little small, rural restaurant that sat about ten to fifteen people. It was a nice place to rest before they took the more than four-hour road trip back to Kato's home. He had gotten his degree, became a children's therapist, and moved to Pinewood, Florida, about 25 minutes away from Miami. He had a nice house, a great career, and no children.

As they walked into the restaurant, they went over to the bar and ordered their food. Tiu-Loo scanned the menu and saw exactly what he wanted. He wanted to try something new, so he asked the waitress if he could have the chocolate and strawberry milkshake blended. The young lady didn't see a problem with it, but she wanted to make sure that it was okay. "Wait, let me get my manager for you, sir," she said. After a few minutes had gone by, a beautiful, green-eyed woman with red hair approached the bar to assist Tiu-Loo. As he turned around, the woman recognized who he was.

"Oh my god, Tiu-Loo! Is that you!?" she shouted.

Tiu-Loo tried to make out who she was, but he couldn't remember. "I'm sorry, but do I know you?" he asked. She explained to him that he and Professor Hunt had produced a play called "Tek Weh Yuself." Tiu-Loo had been one of the judges at her audition. She had beaten Laziah for the part of the French Maid. "I'm Notrice! You remember me?" she asked. "Oh wow! It is you!" he said, as they embraced each other tightly.

Kato was thrown off; he had no idea who Notrice was. He figured their connection had to be related to the theatre class, since she had mentioned it. He introduced Notrice to Kato, and she stood there talking with him. They were only about an hour away from Florida A&T. Notrice had just graduated from college over the summer. Her major of course, was theatre. She had been working at the small restaurant for a few months to earn some extra cash. She was on her way to New York after Christmas to star in a new sitcom that was slated for release the following summer.

She apologized to Tiu-Loo for the things that he had gone through. She was one of the individuals who defended him. Notrice refused to believe that Tiu-Loo had done the things that the media had accused him of. She also thanked him for helping her get the part in his play. She explained to him that she probably wouldn't have taken acting seriously, had he not given her the opportunity. "No, you did that all on your own. You were just the better person for the part," he said, as the waitress brought out his food and blended milkshake.

189

He thanked Notrice for her kind words and told her that he was immensely proud of her and her accomplishments. "This meal is on the house. Enjoy it hun," Notrice said. Tiu-Loo and Kato devoured their plates. There wasn't a speck of food left when they were done. After thanking Notrice for her hospitality, Tiu-Loo and Kato were on their way. The trip was quiet for the most part. They listened to the music and occasionally, Tiu-Loo would rub his bracelet. He hadn't been able to wear it for years due to his incarceration. Upon release, that was one of the first items that had been given back to him.

When they made it to Kato's house, Tiu-Loo was stunned. He had a beautiful two-story home, with a two-car garage. "Damn, bro. You sellin' drugs or what?" Tiu-Loo said, as they entered Kato's place. "Your room is upstairs, boy-boy. Make yourself at home," Kato said. Tiu-Loo was amazed at how his room was put together. Once Kato knew that there had been a possibility for Tiu-Loo's early release, he immediately got to work. There were many trophies and newspaper articles that sat on top of the dresser in his room. He had a large, flatscreen television that had been mounted on the wall for him. His bed was a California King size with soft sheets on it. He was more than satisfied with what he had seen so far.

As Kato was coming upstairs to check on Tiu-Loo, he spotted a picture frame that was located on his nightstand. Inside the frame was a picture of himself and Uncle Kobe, right after he had just qualified for the Olympics. Kato walked into the room and asked, "You need anything, boy-boy?" Tiu-Loo stared long and hard at the picture. He could remember the event like it was yesterday. His uncle was so proud of him, and he had done so much to make sure he could be there to support him.

Tiu-Loo sat on the bed, pulled the picture close to him, and began to cry. The hurt and pain had been too much for him to bare. In many ways, he had blamed himself for Uncle Kobe's death. He felt that if he hadn't gotten into trouble, then maybe Uncle Kobe would've still been alive. Kato went over to console him; he understood what Tiu-Loo had been feeling. He lost the only father figure he'd ever had in his life. Kato also looked up to Uncle Kobe. He was very instrumental in persuading him to choose psychology as his major in college.

"It's so messed up man. It just ain't right, bro," Tiu-Loo said, as Kato sat down beside him. He let Tiu-Loo deal with his emotions and stayed there with him, until he knew that he was okay. Tiu-Loo had been grieving for quite some time now. Therapy could possibly assist him, but Kato didn't want to bring it up anytime soon. He wanted Tiu-Loo to get himself settled and enjoy his freedom for a while. Kato got up and went downstairs. He told Tiu-Loo to let him know if he needed anything. That night, Tiu-Loo stayed up, thinking about his uncle and the countless lessons that he had taught him.

The next morning, Kato had one of his lady friends

prepare breakfast for him and Tiu-Loo. The aroma of freshly cooked bacon, eggs, French toast, and grits made Tiu-Loo rise from his bed with an instant appetite. As he made it downstairs, he could see that Kato had been up for some time. "What's up, boy-boy? Grab a plate," Kato said, as he sat at the kitchen table. He introduced Tiu-Loo to his friend, and she walked into his bedroom. Tiu-Loo made his plate and stood at the counter as he ate his food. He was nearly done before Kato asked him to take a seat.

Tiu-Loo was still adjusting to being a free man. He had become accustomed to eating his food rapidly, while still watching his surroundings. When he sat at the table with Kato, they discussed what he planned to do in the future. Although the state was going to clear his record, he still needed to generate a source of income. Kato suggested that he continued his education to get his degree, but Tiu-Loo wasn't feeling that idea. Anything dealing with school or college had left a sour taste in his mouth. He always felt that being in college was the reason why he ended up in his situation to begin with. He didn't know what he wanted to do as it pertained to work, but he did make a personal request.

"Let's go back to Bama, bro. I just wanna see my old home, one last time," Tiu-Loo said. He hadn't been to Alabama in nearly five years. He wanted to visit the home he had been raised in, and most importantly, he wanted to pay his respects to Uncle Kobe. "That doesn't sound like a bad idea. We'll leave this weekend if you want," Kato replied. Tiu-Loo nodded his head and ate the rest of his food. He wondered how things would be once he stepped foot in Alabama.

Once they made it to their hometown, they could tell that not much had changed. The stores and schools were still the same. The only major difference was the brand-new shopping mall that had been under construction in the downtown district. They did a little sight-seeing before stopping by Tiu-Loo's old home. As he stood in front of the house, he could see that it had been painted another color, and a new family was currently occupying it.

Uncle Kobe had put in his will that one of his brothers could have the house, if something was to happen to him. His brother didn't want to sell the house. Instead, he remodeled it, and started renting it out to qualified tenants. That way, he could generate money, while keeping the property in the family. Uncle Kobe left money and real estate property for Tiu-Loo, that he would be able to have access to when he turned 25. He was incarcerated at the age of nineteen and would soon be turning 24 on his next birthday. He didn't care about any of those things. If he could trade it all to get his uncle back, that's what he would've done.

He and Kato made it to the gravesite where Uncle Kobe had been buried. Kato told him that he had a beautiful homegoing celebration. People from all over came out in droves to pay their respects to Uncle Kobe. He was well-known, respected, and beloved by many of his peers in the community. As he approached his tombstone, Tiu-Loo dropped to his knees. He read the words that were inscribed and sat there quietly for a few minutes. Kato also said a few words. He hadn't been to the gravesite since the funeral. "I love you Uncle Kobe. I promise I'll keep your legacy alive," he said. He hugged the tombstone and rubbed his hand across Uncle Kobe's name.

Tiu-Loo was finally able to see where his uncle had been laid to rest. He was happy to be able to pay his respects, but he still wasn't quite at peace with himself just yet. Nevertheless, he had achieved what he had sat out to do. Within the next 24 hours, he and Kato were on the highway and headed back to Florida. They laughed and talked about their many experiences while growing up in their old neighborhood. That was the first time that Tiu-Loo had been able to free his mind completely, since being released from prison.

As the weeks went by, Tiu-Loo became more familiar with his newfound city he resided in. He would run for a mile or two and complete his 300 pushups and sit-ups right after. He had applied for a few jobs, but no one had given him an opportunity. Every now and then, he would pick up odd jobs that he'd find while reading the back of one of the local newspapers. One day, there was a job listing that required the moving of an elderly woman's furniture. When Tiu-Loo arrived at the home, the woman's grandson answered the door. When Tiu-Loo walked in, the man recognized who he was. "Wait, you're the track star that was accused of raping the girl, right?" the man asked. Tiu-Loo didn't know what to say. Although it had been broadcasted on television, Tiu-Loo wasn't prepared for the attention he would receive from the story.

He stood there calmly and answered the man. "Yes, it was me, unfortunately," Tiu-Loo replied. The man lowered his voice and asked Tiu-Loo to step back outside with him. "Hey man, I know you were found not guilty and all, but my grandmother is an old white lady. Her views are a little different if you know what I mean," the man said. He didn't take offense to his statement, but Tiu-Loo understood the magnitude of his reality. The perception and picture of him had already been painted into the minds of many people years prior to his release. He was aware that if the lie was more entertaining than the truth, then people would certainly believe the lie.

Tiu-Loo excused himself and proceeded to walk away from the man. As he walked off, the man stopped Tiu-Loo. "Wait, here you go. A little something for your trouble. My apologies again, man," he said. He handed Tiu-Loo a 50-dollar bill and walked back into the home. Tiu-Loo had mixed feelings as he made it back to his house. He felt insulted, but grateful at the same time. The man didn't have to give him anything at all, but he did anyway. He didn't like that fact that he was still seen as a villain when it had been proven that he wasn't. He went upstairs and decided to take a long, hot shower. He stood in one spot for nearly an hour, before he began to bathe. His encounter earlier had been heavy on his mind.

It was the second week of December, and Tiu-Loo had received some good news from his lawyer, Ms. Gorman. She informed him that while they couldn't prove that Emilio and Laziah were guilty of setting him up, authorities did want to bring them in for questioning. Tiu-Loo always felt that they were behind his downfall, and now, he was one step closer to finding out. He was anxious to know what had occurred that night, and how he ended up with drugs in his system. Being the fierce and determined lawyer that she was, Tiu-Loo had no doubt that Ms. Gorman would get to the bottom of things in no time.

There was a lot happening that week. Many organizations were getting prepared to hold annual functions for the upcoming events that were taking place on Miami Beach. Kato had mentioned them to Tiu-Loo, but at the time, he wasn't really interested in attending. Once he had received the news from Ms. Gorman, Tiu-Loo found himself to be in a better mood. When Kato made it home from work, he asked if he still had been interested in going to the beach. With no hesitation, Kato grabbed his swimwear and the two of them were on their way.

The skies were clear as they walked on the strip. Different women would wink their eyes and try to take pictures with the two of them every few minutes. Tiu-Loo and Kato had nice figures due to their intensive workout regimens. "I see you still got 'em goin' crazy, boy-boy," Kato said, as they continued to enjoy the view. There were so many different people at the beach. Tiu-Loo had never seen such an incredible mixture of people in one setting. He met different women while competing at the Olympic Trials, but none of them had been wearing bathing suits.

Further down the strip stood a mini stage, that looked like it was being prepared for a presentation. There were American flags all around it. Beside the stage stood a couple of young men who were holding signs with big words that read, "Vote Tom Forde for Congress." A small news crew pulled to the rear of the stage and began reporting on the event. By the time Kato and Tiu-Loo had gotten closer, a tall, dark-skinned man was walking on the stage. He was a slim man with a low haircut. Both of his ears were pierced, and he held a small notepad in his hands. He was sporting a white, tailored suit and looked to be in his mid-30s. As he walked on stage, the crowd began to chant his name. "Tom Forde! Tom Forde! Tom Forde!" He held his hands up to silence them.

He had been elected to run for Congress and was doing one of his many campaigns in the heart of Miami Beach. He spoke clearly and directly to the crowd. He carefully looked through his notes, while explaining the changes he had planned to make within the city. His speech was well received by the crowd, as they clapped loudly and chanted his name once more. Before concluding his speech, he had one more announcement to make. "Thank you all for coming out today. As you all know, I'll be getting married next year. I would like to welcome my beautiful bride to be to the stage," he said.

The young lady walked on stage, and Kato couldn't believe it. "Aw, hell no!" he said. Tiu-Loo had been caught off guard as well. It was Laziah. She was wearing a green dress that fit her body perfectly. She walked on stage to greet her fiancé. He tried to hug her, but she moved her head so that he connected with her cheek instead. She grabbed the microphone and said a few words to the crowd. Tiu-Loo stood there with his arms folded. His mind was roaming all over the place. She, too, had thanked the many supporters that were in the crowd. When she finished talking, she turned the attention back over to Mr. Forde.

"Nah, that chick is foul, boy-boy!" Kato said. Tiu-Loo couldn't have agreed more. Kato went into detail about what Laziah had been up to. When she graduated from college, she became a nude model for a well-known agency in Miami. After a few photoshoots, she disappeared from the scene. One evening, Kato had been trying to search for exotic dancers to book his co-worker's bachelor party. He was told to go on a website called "Friend of a Friend." There were different categories on the site to satisfy different needs and wants. After selecting the dancers, Kato decided to look at the other categories. It didn't surprise him when he saw that Laziah was listed in the "Private Escorts" category. She was more than willing to offer all three of her holes for the going rate of 400 "roses."

Apparently, her fiancé had been oblivious to her past and her present because Kato had just seen her profile on the website two days ago. Not that he had any doubt that Tiu-Loo was innocent of the things she had accused him of, but seeing her profile, on top of his encounter with her in college, gave him all the confirmation that he needed. Tiu-Loo had heard all that he needed to hear. "Maybe I can present this information to my lawyer," he said. Kato told him that it was worth a shot and asked if Tiu-Loo was ready to leave.

As they were about to exit the beach, the crowd once again became loud. Tom Forde had a special guest, who had also turned out to be one of his biggest sponsors. The man walked through the crowd, as he met Mr. Ford in the middle of the stage. "Ladies and gentlemen, our very own Olympic Silver Medalist, Emilio!" he announced, as the crowd went wild with excitement. Indeed, Emilio had become a hometown hero after his achievements at the Olympics. He had been given major endorsement deals for sports drinks and cereal companies.

He had garnered millions of fans worldwide, and even had a sandwich named after him at one of the most popular restaurants in town. He could hardly go into any establishment without someone asking for pictures, autographs, or the occasional request to marry their daughter. The older women would joke with him because of a reality show that he starred in, where he had gone on a quest to find true love. Of, course the ratings were high, but the premise and basis of the show were completely fictional. He had given Tom Forde a large sum of money to endorse his campaign.

Tiu-Loo's body started to tense up. Seeing Emilio receiving the praise and accolades from the people caused him to become upset. "I need to talk to him," Tiu-Loo said, as he started walking towards the stage. Kato tried to stop him, but it was too late. Tiu-Loo had taken off and was already close to the front row. Emilio walked off the stage and was accompanied by two bodyguards. When he saw Tiu-Loo, he immediately had security intervene. "Hey, don't let him come near me!" he said, as one of them halted Tiu-Loo in his steps.

"It's all good, I just wanna have a word with you, homie," Tiu-Loo said, as he smirked at Emilio. He explained to his bodyguards that he wasn't there to cause trouble. In fact, he only wanted to catch up and have a brief discussion. Seeing the commotion, Laziah walked off the stage to assist Emilio. "So, you stalkin' my cousin, now? You need to get a life!" she said while helping Emilio's security team move him to his vehicle. "Chick, don't flatter yourself," Tiu-Loo said, while still attempting to make it over to Emilio.

Kato had finally caught up with him and tried to pull him away from the crowd. "Let's go, boy-boy. This shit ain't even worth it," he said, as he successfully got Tiu-Loo to calm down. The bodyguards asked them both to leave while they got everything under control. Laziah and Emilio laughed at Tiu-Loo, as he became visibly enraged during the dispute. "It won't be funny for long. After they bring yo ass in for questioning," Kato said. He was well aware of the cops wanting to question Laziah and Emilio. He knew that the truth would come out eventually.

"Yea, and my lawyers will eat them up for lunch! How 'bout that?!" Emilio replied. Mr. Forde grabbed Laziah and asked her to calm down. He didn't want her to be seen in a negative light; a belligerent woman on the arms of a well-established congressman, was not the ideal image that he wanted to be portrayed in the eyes of potential voters. Laziah walked over to the vehicle that Emilio was in and gave him a hug. Seeing that Tiu-Loo was still fuming from the altercation, they threw one more jab at him. "Maybe those pills are making him lose his mind a little bit," Emilio said, as he and Laziah laughed hysterically.

"The fuck you just say?!" Tiu-Loo shouted, attempting to rush Emilio once again. Kato grabbed him and walked him through the crowd. "Alright, that's enough," Mr. Forde said. He had gotten irritated and was tired of seeing Laziah act like a child. As he tried to grab her hand, she snatched away from him. He put on a fake smile and held his head down, as he tried to mask his obvious embarrassment.

When they made it home, Kato decided to order pizza. "You good, boy-boy?" he asked Tiu-Loo. He was extremely frustrated. Seeing Emilio and Laziah only heightened his anger and hate for them. "Yea, I'm good, bro. I'm 'bout to head upstairs," Tiu-Loo replied. Kato told him that he would let him know when the pizza arrived.

Tiu-Loo opened one of the books that had been given to him while he was in prison. Each night, he would read about the different types of murders that had been committed throughout history. He grabbed his laptop from his dresser and looked up the website that Kato had told him about at the beach. When he looked at the categories, the first profile he saw was Laziah's. He also discovered that she went by the name of "Accent" on the site. He studied her likes and dislikes and made a mental note. After storing her online number in his phone, he made a promising remark. "It's time to end this shit!" he said, as he shut his laptop down.

Chapter 11: Sweet Revenge

For three whole months, he studied his every move. There was an early morning jog at 8 am. He dropped his son off at the babysitter by 10 am, lunch by noon, and home with his family by 3:30 pm, Monday through Friday. His weekends were spent differently. On the first and third weekends of the month, he would meet with different promotors and career planners. On the second and fourth weekends, he would convince his wife that he had a mandatory meeting with his business partner. However, these meetings would just be a cover up to go out on expensive dates with his mistress, Becca.

Tiu-Loo had already mapped out the time and day; all he had to do was execute his plan. As Kato walked into the house, he handed Tiu-Loo his mail. He had been waiting on some particularly important documents. "Here you go, boy-boy," Kato said, as he opened the refrigerator door. Tiu-Loo was anxious. He opened the two envelopes and there they were. His visa and passport had finally arrived. "Bout time!" Tiu-Loo said. Seeing the world was something that he had been wanting to do for quite some time.

After Kato told him about his trip to the Bahamas the year before, he convinced Tiu-Loo to apply for the documents and to travel the world. He saw that Tiu-Loo was excited about receiving his new passport. "So, where you plan on traveling to?" Kato asked. "I have a place in mind, but I'll wait until it's the right time to visit," Tiu-Loo replied. Kato was curious to know where Tiu-Loo had been planning on going, since he hadn't mentioned anything recently. As they talked in the living room, a breaking news alert appeared on the television screen.

It was an exclusive interview featuring Emilio. After taking a year off from track and field, he announced that he would be competing in the long jump competition that had been scheduled for the next month in Japan. "You see this shit, boy-boy?" Kato asked. Tiu-Loo didn't respond. He was quiet as a mouse. He excused himself and went outside to the front yard. Concerned about his friend, Kato followed behind to see if things were okay. He decided not to approach Tiu-Loo, because he could tell that he was trying to clear his head. He was pacing back and forth, staring at the ground, and talking to himself. Whatever had been bothering Tiu-Loo at that moment, was beyond Kato's comprehension. He walked back into the house and let Tiu-Loo vent his frustrations.

As Kato pulled out of the driveway to head to work the next morning, Tiu-Loo was making a phone call to one of the local gun dealers in the city. Yung Gunzo was a gym rat by day and an arsenal expert by night. He could get anything that you wanted for the right price. After sending him the address, Yung Gunzo was at his doorstep within an hour. Formerly a member of one of the most notorious Haitian gangs in Miami, Yung Gunzo changed his life for the better after his twin brother, Khadafi, was killed during a shootout with a rival gang.

He met Tiu-Loo a few weeks prior while running on the beach. He gave him a business card and told Tiu-Loo to contact him whenever he needed assistance. It didn't take long for his services to be requested. He followed Tiu-Loo inside the house, where they sat at the dining room table. Yung Gunzo carried two, large duffle bags over to the couch. He asked if Tiu-Loo knew how to shoot a gun. Tiu-Loo answered his question with a confident yes. He had never physically shot a gun, but his books and research on how to shoot made him feel like he was prepared.

Yung Gunzo asked Tiu-Loo to walk over to the couch with him. He unzipped the two duffle bags and pulled a single gun out of each one of them. One of the guns was a semi-automatic, MAC 11, and the other was a Glock .45 pistol. Tiu-Loo held the Mac in his hands. He liked it, but he felt that it was too bulky for what his plans were. When Yung Gunzo handed him the Glock .45, Tiu-Loo immediately fell in love with it. "This is the one! How much for it?" Tiu-Loo asked. After Yung Gunzo gave him the price, Tiu-Loo went upstairs to get the money.

After handing the cash to Yung Gunzo, he still wasn't sure about selling the gun to Tiu-Loo. He didn't believe that he knew how to handle such a powerful handgun. Kato had a nice sized backyard. Yung Gunzo grabbed a silencer from one of the duffle bags, screwed it to the front of the gun, and asked Tiu-Loo if they could go outside. There were a couple of pallets of sod in the backyard. They had been left behind by one of the landscapers who were supposed to finish their job within the next few days.

Yung Gunzo grabbed one of the beer cans that had been left behind, and he placed it on top of the high pile of sod. "Step back here and shoot this for me," Yung Gunzo said. They stood about 25 yards away from their intended target. Yung Gunzo handed Tiu-Loo the gun and didn't think he would be able to hit the can; Tiu-Loo didn't look like a shooter to him. Tiu-Loo held the gun in his hand and pulled the trigger. It turned out that he was very efficient shooter. On his first try, he hit the can right in the middle, exactly where he was aiming. "Well damn, I didn't think you had it in you. Good shit!" Yung Gunzo said. They walked back into the house, and Yung Gunzo gave Tiu-Loo both the gun and the silencer.

"Preciate this bro," Tiu-Loo said, as Yung Gunzo grabbed the duffle bag that held the MAC 11 inside of it. He let Tiu-Loo keep the other one as a gift for making his purchase. "Be safe and remember, you didn't get that from me," Yung Gunzo said, as Tiu-Loo let him out. Once he took his new gun upstairs, he stood in his mirror. He held his gun the proper way, just like the book had taught him; both hands were steady, with his eyes locked on his target. As he aimed, he controlled his breathing, by slowly exhaling. Tiu-Loo had finally added the last official piece to his puzzle.

He had been pushed to his limit. Tiu-Loo had been beating himself up mentally and emotionally for years. Even as he tried to get his life on track, his past seemed to stunt his progression. He loved Kato; he appreciated everything that he had done for him. But ultimately, like any man, he knew that Kato would want to enjoy the privacy of his home by himself. He had spent four years in prison for a crime that he didn't commit. The two individuals who were clearly responsible for his incarceration, were living their lives and making a mockery of the atrocities that he had to endure. Pissed off, and still grieving over the loss of his dear, Uncle Kobe, Tiu-Loo had reached his breaking point.

It was Saturday, and it was the second weekend of the month. Kato had chosen to spend the night with his lady friend and was going to stay with her until Monday morning. He left his keys and car with Tiu-Loo in case he needed to run errands, while he was gone. Tiu-Loo had already been buying time, as he drove around the city. It was 10:30 pm, and Emilio was with Becca at a rented luxurious townhouse. At 10:45 pm, he would always open the door to bring in a bouquet of flowers that would be dropped off for his mistress. Tiu-Loo had calculated that it had taken approximately 28 seconds for Emilio to open the door, walk to get the flowers, and then head back inside.

It was a quiet community and Tiu-Loo didn't want to look suspicious. At 10:40 pm, Tiu-Loo parked Kato's vehicle in an alley that was two blocks from the location. He ran up to the side of the building where Emilio was located. He was dressed in black from head to toe. His long dreadlocks were covered by his hoodie and the ski-mask that was also shielding his face. The Glock .45 pistol was as black as the gloves that covered his hands. He waited patiently for Emilio to open the door.

He hid behind a small bush that was aligned with the walkway, located outside of the townhouse. It was just the right amount of distance for him to get a running start. He sat still, ensuring that his stealth would help him blend in with the darkness. The porchlight shined, just enough for him to be able to see precisely when the doorknob was moving. He had his gun in his right hand and was kneeling close to the ground as he waited.

Like clockwork, he could see the door began to open. Emilio was walking towards the flowers that were only a few feet away. He adjusted his white robe as he walked. With no time to spare, Tiu-Loo took off running towards him. A solid strike to the forehead of Emilio caused him to hit the ground almost instantaneously. He let out an agonizing groan, as he tried to comprehend what was taking place. "Man, you gotta be aware of your surroundings. Get yo' punk ass up!" Tiu-Loo demanded, as he grabbed the top of Emilio's robe. He put the gun up to his face and led him inside the house.

When they made it into the home, Becca was laying on the couch, half naked. She didn't realize that they had company. When she saw Tiu-Loo, she was about to scream until he pointed the gun at her. "Look, I don't wanna hurt you, but I promise if you make this a loud situation, there will be two dead bodies instead of one," he said. Becca nodded her head, as she understood the seriousness of the situation. Emilio's white robe had now been splattered with a little bit of red. The brutal hit to his forehead caused a gash to form.

There were two chairs in the living room area of the townhouse. Tiu-Loo ordered Becca to sit down in one of them. The tall, Russian model was scared out of her mind. She trembled with fear, as she obeyed Tiu-Loo's commands. Emilio was afraid as well. He immediately began to offer Tiu-Loo money, as he was under the impression that a robbery was taking place. "Nah, I don't want your fuckin money. This is bigger than that," Tiu-Loo said, as he struck Emilio in the face with the gun again.

Emilio put his hands up and begged for mercy. He was clueless and wondered why he was being attacked. Becca cried silently, as she saw the blood coming from Emilio's mouth. There were extension cords on the floor that Emilio had been using earlier. Tiu-Loo made him tie Becca's hands together with one of them. He then made him use his red tie that matched his outfit, as a blindfold to cover Becca's eyes with. After she had been taken care of, Tiu-Loo ordered Emilio to sit down in the second chair.

He had him put his hands behind him, while he tied them tightly with the other extension cord. At this point,

Emilio was afraid for his life. "Please man, please! What is this about?!" He asked, as fear traveled in his voice. Tiu-Loo looked around the house to see if any cameras were present. After Emilio assured him that there weren't any, he began to talk to him. "You thought I was just gonna let that shit slide, huh?" Tiu-Loo asked Emilio, as he interrogated him. Emilio tried to reason with him. He told him that he had the wrong house, and that he promised he wouldn't say anything if he would just let them go.

Tiu-Loo laughed at Emilio. It was funny hearing him beg for mercy. He was such a cocky and unappreciative individual. Hearing Emilio beg for his life was gratifying, but he was tired of toying with him. He was there for one reason, and one reason only. "Just know, that you brought this on yourself. I'll see you on the other side, frat boy" Tiu-Loo said. Before he could pull the trigger, Emilio stopped him. "Wait, who are you? Please man, I have a son and a wife at home," he said, as he began to cry. Tiu-Loo became even more enraged. There was never any accountability being held on Emilio's end. He stepped on others to get ahead, and even with a very faithful wife at home, he was committing the ultimate betrayal by cheating on her.

"You don't give a damn about your wife! You fuckin THIEF! Does she know that you've spent almost half a million dollars on this chick!?" Tiu-Loo asked. He had all his information correct. Over the course of two years, Emilio had spent nearly 500,000 dollars on Becca. They took expensive vacations, went shopping at fancy stores, and he even paid for her breast and buttocks to be enhanced. Becca kept quiet; she knew that Emilio had a family, but it didn't matter, as long as he continued to support and spoil her. He tried to plead his case, but Tiu-Loo had heard enough. "Fuck that! I'm tired of talkin!" he said, as he aimed the gun at Emilio's head.

He let off three shots, and the room was silent. Becca didn't make a sound, but was shaking with fear, as she heard Tiu-Loo's footsteps coming towards her. She could tell that something bad had happened because Emilio wasn't talking anymore. There wasn't a loud bang from the gun because the silencer was on it. When he walked over to her, he removed the tie from her eyes, and untied her hands. "I'm not gonna hurt you, okay? He was a bad man. He had it coming," he said. After telling her to call the cops, Tiu-Loo calmly walked out of the house. Emilio's body was slumped over. The two bullets in his chest didn't cause much damage, but the one in his head ended his life for sure.

When Tiu-Loo made it outside, he ran back to the alley where he had parked Kato's car. The coast was clear. He removed his ski-mask and clothing immediately. He placed his gun into the duffle bag that he brought with him as well. Once his clothes had been replaced, he pulled off like any other normal civilian in the neighborhood. His heart was beating rapidly, as he drove back home. He kept his composure as much as he could, but whenever a police car would pass by, he couldn't help but to think that he was about to get pulled over. Every minute felt like an hour while he was driving. Although he had just committed murder, he was concerned for Becca.

He had every intent on causing harm to Emilio, but Becca just happened to be in the wrong place at the wrong time. He finally made it home, and parked Kato's car in the garage. He didn't want to get out of the car just yet. While carefully looking around the inside of the vehicle, he made sure that nothing of his was left behind. Tiu-Loo walked to the back of the car and removed the black piece of tape from the license plate. He had placed it there, before he left home; if someone were to identify Kato's vehicle, neither them nor the cops would be able to tell who it belonged to.

He went upstairs to his room and put the duffle bag into his closet. There were many thoughts in his head, but he stayed the course. He took his clothes off and sat on his bed. All he could think about was the fear in Emilio's eyes before he pulled the trigger. Tiu-Loo was glad that he was dead. He didn't rejoice nor celebrate, but he was surely satisfied with what he had done. There was no sorrow, no pain, and certainly no remorse. He had successfully carried out a well, thought out and planned execution.

The following week had been a tumultuous one for friends, family, and fans all over the state of Florida. The city of Miami mourned the tragic passing of Emilio. There were murals being painted, and millions of people gathered at his gravesite to honor his legacy and the many things he had achieved in his life. The Miami Police Department had no idea why someone would want to kill him. He had created a foundation for underprivileged children, he was a mentor, and he supported local businesses in every way that he could. They had no leads on his murder case, and all Becca could tell them was that a man wearing all black, forced his way into the home, and ultimately took Emilio's life.

There were a ton of celebrities at his funeral. Many basketball and football athletes spoke at his eulogy. Even the President of the Dominican Republic had made a special appearance. There were so many people hurting and left in the dark about why Emilio met such a horrific fate. There were awards of up to 50,000 dollars for anyone who may have had information about the events that led up to Emilio's death. While doing a press conference, the police chief made a promise to capture each and every perpetrator that had been involved in the crime. Miami's streets had become restless.

Although Kato and Emilio didn't see eye to eye, he never wished death on him. He found himself asking questions as to what may have made someone want to actually kill him. When he came home from work one afternoon, he had a brief talk with Tiu-Loo. "Man, a shot to the head? That shit was personal," he said, as Tiu-Loo sat at the kitchen table eating a bowl of cereal. He was aware of how drastically the climate had changed in the city, and he was the reason for it. "Yea, that's crazy," Tiu-Loo replied, as he scooped another bite into his mouth.

213

Before Kato left the room, Tiu-Loo told him that he would be leaving soon. He had found another place to stay, and there wouldn't be too many more days left to spend with each other. It took Kato by surprise. "What's goin' on? Is everything alright, boy-boy?" Kato asked. Tiu-Loo laughed it off and told him that it was just time for him to get his own place. He had a job waiting for him, and he would earn enough money that would enable him to take care of and support himself. Kato insisted that he stay there. He liked having Tiu-Loo around, and there was more than enough space for him at his house. He didn't know what was going on, but Tiu-Loo wanting to leave so suddenly just didn't sit well with him. Yet and still, he understood where Tiu-Loo was coming from with his logic.

A month had gone by, and Emilio's death seemed to be a thing of the past for most people. He still had fans who visited his house and gravesite. Many of them went to the famous restaurant and ordered the sandwich that had been named after him. The internet had been buzzing, as many individuals talked about their personal experiences with him, and how he impacted their lives. Most of the feedback had been positive on his behalf. Emilio had die-hard fans who would've done almost anything for him.

Mr. Tom Forde had done his best to console his fiancé. Laziah had taken the news of her cousin's death extremely hard. There were nights where she wouldn't eat. Already lacking the ability to show affection, Emilio's death caused her to nearly shut down completely. She used his death as an excuse to be an even more sadistic woman to the one man who really had her back. It seemed that nothing Mr. Forde ever did, was satisfactory enough for her standards. All the shoes, money, and purses in the world could never compete with her selfish and malicious ways. She was a completely self-centered and aggressive individual.

There were times when she would purposely start an argument with Mr. Forde, just to go out and have a fling with another man. The money that she had come into because of her relationship with him, only heightened the cruel and shallow person that she already was. However, things were about to change very soon. Before Emilio died, he had revised his will. Laziah was to be given ten percent of the next endorsement check that Emilio had received. Two days before his death, he paid half of the one million dollars that was owed to him. He had just finished shooting a commercial for a brand name shoe company. After he did his part, they would pay his additional amount within 60 days of the contract agreement. Laziah had a 100,000-dollar check coming her way in less than 30 days. She was planning on leaving Tom Forde for this mysterious guy that she had met on the Friend of a Friend website.

He talked about how he would take care of her, and that he was the heir to his late father's oil company. They had been texting and chatting for several months. His pictures looked good to her, and he had money. In Laziah's book, he was a complete package. She set up a date to meet with him on a Friday afternoon, but she wanted him to pick the time and place. She was eager to get next to this mysterious man, who simply went by the name, "Q." Mr. Forde tried desperately to show Laziah how much he loved her, but she was never receptive to his attempts. She had a mean streak that just wouldn't allow her to have a heart. She was far more, worse than Emilio when it came to getting what she wanted.

After a long week of work, Kato decided that it was time to do something fun for a change. He noticed that Tiu-Loo hadn't been on a date or in the company of a woman since he'd been released from prison. He joked with him the night before about becoming a born-again virgin. They always clowned each other whenever they could. A lot of the laughter they shared together had been the key component to keeping Tiu-Loo grounded and sane.

Kato turned his music on and began cleaning his house. He had invited two young women over to hang with him and Tiu-Loo. As he swept his kitchen floor, he noticed that Tiu-Loo hadn't come downstairs yet. When he went to see what Tiu-Loo was up to, he thought he had been invited to a concert. Tiu-Loo had on a pair of blue slacks, a nice button-down shirt, and a pair of dress shoes. Kato put his hand over his mouth and was impressed by the way Tiu-Loo had put himself together. "Okay now, boy-boy! I see you," Kato said, as he walked around Tiu-Loo, giving him his stamp of approval.

"I was gonna ask if I could use the car tonight. I got

a hot date," Tiu-Loo said. Kato was blown away. Not only was his buddy dressed to impress, but he was also going out with someone. "You know what, I had a couple ladies coming through to entertain us, but I think I can handle both of them," Kato said. He was happy to see that Tiu-Loo was getting out of the house for once. It was a nice, Friday afternoon, and the weather outside was feeling good. Tiu-Loo grabbed his duffle bag and went downstairs to get the keys to Kato's car.

It was nearing 5:30 pm, and Kato had received a text from the young ladies. They were eight minutes away and Tiu-Loo was about to leave to meet with his date. He and Kato had been conversing for a couple of hours about random topics. They would do that from time to time, whenever Kato wasn't busy with work. Before he walked out of the house, Tiu-Loo expressed his gratitude to Kato. "I really wanna thank you for allowing me to stay here, bro. You'll never know how much that means to me. I'm gonna miss you when I leave," he said, as he began to become emotional. They shook hands and embraced each other.

"No need to cry, boy-boy. It's not like you're leaving tomorrow," Kato said. Tiu-Loo hugged him even tighter when he heard those words. Once the embrace was over, Tiu-Loo wiped the one tear that fell down his face. Kato told him to be safe, and to enjoy his night. Tiu-Loo picked up his duffle bag and went into the garage to start the car. "And please get laid while you're out tonight," Kato said, as he pushed the button to let his garage door down. Tiu-Loo laughed as he drove away. He was ready for his "date night."

He had given his date the address to meet him. Because she had explained to him that she was involved with a very prestigious man, Tiu-Loo picked a discreet location for them to meet. Yung Gunzo had been working on opening a private gym for his new clients, but he wasn't quite ready to complete the project. He had the building already, but there was no furniture or electricity. It was the perfect place for privacy though. Tiu-Loo parked Kato's car on the side of the street near a park. He pulled his black hoodie out of his duffle bag and put it on. The sun was just starting to go down. In order to keep a low profile, Tiu-Loo opted to walk the extra ten minutes that it had taken to make it to his destination.

Once he arrived at the building, he opened the door and let himself in. There was no lock, which made it easy for him to gain entry. He already had his black gloves on, ensuring that no fingerprints were being left behind. There was a large table in the middle of the main room. Tiu-Loo pulled two candles from his bag. He placed them on top of the table after he lit them. He had the bottle of wine that his date had requested; she would be arriving shortly. He pulled out a chair for her to sit in when she got there. Although the candles were lit, it was still fairly dark inside the building.

Within the next few minutes, Tiu-Loo's date was walking into the establishment. She didn't want her significant other to be skeptical about her whereabouts, so she devised a plan that she felt would outsmart him. She had one of her girlfriends pick her up and drop her off. The plan was to stay for a few hours, and then make the phone call when she was ready to leave. As she walked into the building, everything was dark except the lights from the candles. "Ms. Accent, nice to finally meet you," Tiu-Loo said. She could see a person moving but couldn't see his face. "Nice to meet you too, but I can't see where I'm going," she replied. "Just follow the light, love," Tiu-Loo said, as she got closer.

He continued to guide her with his voice. He had his back turned as he continued to talk. As she got closer to the table, she could see that he remembered to get her the bottle of wine. "You're so sweet for doing this. I know we're gonna have a good time," she said. When she sat down in the chair, Tiu-Loo turned around, with his gun in his hand. Accent's heart suddenly started to feel like it wasn't beating inside her chest anymore. She couldn't believe that it was him the whole time. Before she could even scream, Tiu-Loo had made it around the table with the gun pointed to her face.

"Please…. please don't shoot me, Tiu-Loo!" she said, as her legs began to shake violently. His finger was on the trigger, but he didn't want to pull it. "Nah, you're not even worth a bullet," he replied. He removed the top from his hoodie to reveal his face in its entirety to her. He began to question her about the reasons that her and Emilio set him up. "I just wanna know why. What the fuck did I do to you to make you ruin my life the way you did?" Tiu-Loo asked. As she began to cry, she explained to him that she felt slighted by him. He felt like he was better than everyone else, and her cousin despised him. Tiu-Loo didn't want to hear it.

"Aw naw, you gotta do better than that, Laziah, 'cause 'Ms. Accent' ain't makin' sense right now," he replied. After Kato had given him the name of the website that she was on, he stored her number and began texting her. He told her that his name was "Q" and made up a story about his life as they continued to talk to one another. When she began asking him to send pictures of himself, he downloaded pictures of a male model off the internet. He pretended that they were images of him. He had completely fooled Laziah into thinking that she was about to start a new life with the heir of an oil tycoon. He hated Laziah the most. Her smart mouth and evil personality made him want to smack her.

"I'm sorry for what we did to you, Tiu-Loo, I really am," Laziah said, as she continued to cry. She didn't know if he was going to shoot her, or actually try to sexually assault her. As she tried to get through to Tiu-Loo, he started to talk about what he had gone through since being sent to prison. "Nah BITCH! You're not a victim! Tell me, do you know what it feels like to lose everything you've ever worked for? To have to fight for your life every single day in prison.... or to lose the one person that loved you unconditionally? Do you!? I lost my fuckin uncle because of your lies and your games. So, what are the consequences of that, huh? How do we fix this? Oh, that's right, we can't, because my uncle's DEAD, you triflin' ass BITCH!"

The roar in his voice made Laziah nearly jump out of the chair that she was sitting in. While pointing the gun at her, Tiu-Loo backed up towards the table to retrieve his duffle bag. He opened it and pulled out a medium sized plastic bag, and a large role of grey duct tape. He walked over to Laziah and made her put her hands behind the chair. He grabbed her hands and taped them together tightly. He then put both of her legs together, and tied them together, while adding a few more layers to the bottom of the chair.

Tears flowed like a river as she realized that her life may be ending soon. "Look, I can get you whatever you want. Is it money or what? You don't have to do this," Laziah said, still attempting to persuade Tiu-Loo to rethink his plan. His mind had already been made up. To him, she was a complete danger to the community, and for that, she had to go. "This shit is bigger than money, Laziah. And what I want... money simply can't buy," Tiu-Loo replied. He stood over her and cocked his gun. "Please, don't shoot me," Laziah pleaded. He kept a straight face, as he sat his gun on the table.

He grabbed the plastic bag and stood behind her. Tiu-Loo made one last statement. "I told you, you ain't worth a bullet, but you definitely gone die. You trash ass bitch!" He placed the bag over Laziah's face. He pulled it tightly to her skin and tied a knot into it. Once he saw that the back was completely covering her face and neck, he grabbed the duct tape. Tiu-Loo wrapped the duct tape in several layers, covering her entire neck and mouth. He made sure that no air was able to come out of the bag. Her eyes rolled into the back of her head, as she struggled to breathe. She tried to move her arms and kick her feet, but the duct tape was entirely too strong, and Tiu-Loo made sure of it.

She put up a good fight for the first 65 seconds, but by the time Tiu-Loo had seen the three-minute mark on his phone, Laziah had stopped moving altogether. He waited another five minutes to make sure no other movement would occur. There was no doubt about her current state; she was dead, and he was done. He covered his head with his hoodie, loaded the items back into his duffle bag, and left the building. Once he made it back the car, he repeated the same routine that he did after he had killed Emilio. He made sure that he took Laziah's phone with him also. He didn't want any traces of evidence to lead back to him.

He had been using another phone to contact Laziah, which enabled him to do away with the one that he had been using. Before he completed his trip home, he drove to a river. He took both of their phones and slammed them on the ground until they shattered into pieces. After that, he threw the components into the water, along with his Glock .45 pistol. When he made it back home, he stayed outside in the driveway. He could hear the music playing and could tell that Kato was enjoying the ladies and their company. He waited until he knew Kato had gone into his bedroom, before he entered the house.

By the time Tiu-Loo had made it to his bedroom, it was 4:30 am. He removed his clothes and walked downstairs. He opened the cabinet under the sink to grab a large, trash bag. After putting all his clothing into the bag, Tiu-Loo took it outside to place it in the dumpster. He ran upstairs and packed a large suitcase. He only took a few articles of clothing with him. After placing the portrait of himself and Uncle Kobe into his suitcase, he made his way to the living room. He cracked Kato's door to see if he was awake, but he knew that he wasn't. He was sandwiched between two naked women. The liquor on his dresser suggested that the night had been a success. They were all sound asleep. Tiu-Loo shook his head and smiled, as he closed his bedroom door quietly.

He grabbed a pen and paper, to write a short letter to Kato. "My dear brother. I thank you for your words and your hospitality. Take care of yourself, boy-boy," It was 6:25 am, and it was beginning to light up outside. Tiu-Loo called a cab to come get him. Once the cab driver arrived, he took one last look at the house. He closed the door and locked it behind him. Once he put his suitcase into the trunk, Tiu-Loo was gone. As he sat in the back of the taxi, another breaking news report was being announced on the radio. Laziah's body had been found dead. Her girlfriend had been calling her all night. When she didn't hear from her, she alerted the authorities. Tiu-Loo sat back and asked the driver to change the station.

When he arrived at the airport, he saw that he was an

hour early. As he prepared to check his suitcase in with security, he could hear the announcements on the speaker system. "All passengers boarding the flight to Havana, Cuba, please report to Gate 22 please," the announcer said. Tiu-Loo grabbed his cellphone and made a phone call. It rang several times before the person answered. "Yo, wassup Asere!?" the man said. "Hello, Gator? What's up, Asere!? I'm on my way to paradise, bro. I'll see you soon!" Tiu-Loo replied. He cleared the security checkpoint successfully and sat at the window seat that he had chosen when he purchased his ticket. Seeing the clouds while he was flying in the sky had given him the refreshing feeling of peace and tranquility. Indeed, Tiu-Loo had finally been able to relax.